FONTB

Gotta Get Some
BISH BASH BOSH

Gotta Get Some
BISH BASH
BOSH

M. E. ALLEN

Katherine Tegen Books
An Imprint of HarperCollins*Publishers*

Gotta Get Some Bish Bash Bosh
Copyright © 2005 by M. E. Allen
A paperback edition of this book was published in
the United Kingdom in 2003 by Egmont Books.
For information address HarperCollins Children's Books,
a division of HarperCollins Publishers,
1350 Avenue of the Americas,
New York, NY 10019.
www.harpertempest.com

Library of Congress Cataloging-in-Publication Data
Allen, M. E.
Gotta get some bish bash bosh / M. E. Allen.—1st ed.
p.   cm.
Summary: After getting dumped by his girlfriend, a four-
teen-year-old English boy attempts to change his image.
ISBN 0-06-073198-2 — ISBN 0-06-073201-6 (lib. bdg.)
[1. Identity—Fiction.   2. Interpersonal relations—Fiction.
3. Schools—Fiction.   4. England—Fiction.]   I.Title.
PZ7.A4285Go   2005   2004002326
[Fic]—dc22

Typography by Larissa Lawrynenko
1 2 3 4 5 6 7 8 9 10
❖
First U. S. edition, 2005

For Lucy and Gordon,
and special thanks to Cally

Contents

One

Slam-Dumped

IF YOU'RE PLANNING on going out with a girl, take my advice: don't start over the summer holidays. Do it in term time, when there's loads of other distractions. Over the long summer holiday, keeping a girl happy on a day-to-day basis can really drain you. It's nonstop phone calls. Boring shopping trips into town. Coke and cappuccino consumption levels shooting sky high.

Not that I've tired of my girlfriend Sandi or anything. Don't get me wrong. If you want a girlfriend, Sandi's it.

Flipping hard work, though. And soaks up all your dosh.

Brrring-brrring, brrring-brrring . . .

"He-llo," purrs this sexy, girlie voice.

"Sand. . .? That you? Got a mouthful of chocolate? 'S only me. Er . . . Just ringing to—"

"Oh rats—only you?" Her voice turns shrill. Slashes into my train of thought, like a brain surgeon wielding a machete. "I thought it was *him*."

"Er—what? Who?"

She's giggling. And somebody's joining in. Sounds like one of her mates.

"Some bloke at a gym. Just rang. Offering a free session, if you booked in advance for six more. Sounded dead *hunky*. So I put on this deep, sexy voice. Said I'd think about it. So *he* said he'd . . . ring me back!" She collapses into hysterical laughter. The anonymous friend joins in.

I hold the phone away from my ear.

Pathetic! Girls act so dumb sometimes, it makes you squirm. Usually when there's a cluster of two or more of 'em together. I'm surprised at Sandi, though. Giggling girlie stuff's not her style.

"Well, sorry to disappoint you," I say icily. "Some of us prefer to exercise our brains."

Rude snigger. "So what did you want, anyway?"

4

"Who's that with you?"

"Natalie."

Ah. Might have known. Natalie's trouble. That girl could stir up a riot in a bag of marshmallows. I hesitate. I tap a fingernail against my left incisor. Was going to invite Sandi into town. Not going to get lumbered with Natalie as well, though.

"Hello? Still there?" says Sandi.

"Er, just wondering if you fancy coming into town this afternoon? Or if you fancy the park—feeding the ducks. Just *you*," I add.

"Town? Ducks?" Sounds like Sandi's yawning. "To be honest, I'm bored with both. Listen, why don't you come around here? Natalie and I are customizing our flip-flops. You're welcome to bring yours. You have to supply your own materials, though. Buttons, sequins, feathers—whatever expresses your personality." A smothered explosion of cackling breaks out in the background. Natalie's always had it in for me.

"Listen," I grind, "catch me wearing flip-flops, never mind customizing them, and you can send for a straightjacket!" (That's telling them.)

"Well, Mr. Sneery, if you can think of anything more brain stimulating to do . . ."

"Plenty!"

Then I hang up sharp, before Sandi recovers from her choking fit and asks me what.

Brrring-brrring, brrring-brrring . . .

It's my best mate.

"Hi, Ric. What're you doing?"

"Just playing on my PlayStation," he drones. "Wanna come over this afternoon? It's dead boring around here."

Ric's been dumped. He's currently suffering from a dose of terminal self-pity that puts his chances of getting a home visit from me roughly on a par with a victim of the Black Death.

Here's how it goes:

"Still no reply to your latest e-mail?" I ask, in my most considerate tone, to get it over with. "How long since you sent it? Let's see, ten days, is it?"

Snotty sniff. Can't make out if he's saying "eleven" or "seven."

"Best out of it. Girls? Ha! Not worth the grief."

6

"'S all right for you." He sounds so saturated with self-pity, you could wring him out. "You've got Sandi."

"Ah, yeah. Well . . ."

"Remember all the trouble *you* had, getting a girl to go out with you, before Sandi took you on?"

"Took me on!" I splutter. "What ya mean, 'took me *on*'! Other way around, mate! Sandi Weston was lucky to get her graspers on me. Fortunately she knows it."

No sympathizing with kids like Ric, is there? Try, and you end up wanting to wring their scraggy necks instead.

I sink into a smoldering silence. It's just wasted on Ric. Self-obsession's set in again. "It's like when you're not picked for footie," he's groaning. "There's the picked, and then there's you—the unpicked. The leftovers. Rejects. Spares. Guys girls just don't seem to fancy. . ."

Any second now he'll start telling me he's ugly. The subject of his blackheads might arise. Halitosis even.

"Ooops. Phone's beeping. Battery must be going. Can't make it this afternoon. Catch you later. Er— have a good day," I add.

• • •

Brrring-brrring, brrring-brrring . . .

What if that's Ric again?

What if it's somebody interesting?

"Hi. It's Sandi."

"Oh, thought it might be gorgeous, pouting Donna, trying to interest me in her double glazing."

Pause.

"Sorry, did I miss a joke somewhere?" she says.

"So what can I do for you?" I snap.

Sounds like she's taking a deep breath.

"I've made a decision . . ."

"Oh yeah?"

Silence.

"Go on, then. Spit it out." I snap my fingers. "Ah, you've changed your mind. Do wanna go into town. Can't bring yourself to grovel. Okay, so where'll I meet you?"

"I've-decided-I-don't-want-to-go-out-with-you-anymore. Sorry and all that."

The clock's stopped ticking. My blood's stopped flowing. The traffic's all screeched to a halt. The world's suddenly shrouded in silence.

"What?" I croak.

"I've decided—"

"Sand—what're you saying? You mean you're d-dumping me?"

"Er . . . yeah," she says. "It's like this: I used to think you were fun. Only now I've reached the stage where girls start fancying more mature guys. You know, guys with a bit more bish bash bosh."

My blood suddenly starts flowing again. Like red-hot lava.

How dare she dump me? And, what's more, personally insult me. In front of a witness.

What's she mean "more mature"?

What's she mean "more bish bash bosh"?

Aren't I the guy who's forever knocking himself inside out, trying to be slick, stylish, and original?

The injustice seers into me like a branding iron.

I feel pain! I feel hurt! I'm flipping *livid*.

"WHA—T?" I roar down the phone.

Click. She's gone. Coward!

Oooh—can't move. It's like lightning's struck, welding me to the sofa.

I'm dumped. A dumpee. I can't believe it.

I'm back on the bench again, same as Ric.

No! Help! Not like Ric.

I pry myself off the sofa and stomp life back into my limbs. Gotta take action fast, before my self-esteem hits zero. Before I'm caught in the grip of terminal self-pity. Before Ric-ormortis sets in!

I snatch up the phone. I speed dial Sandi's number.

Bish bash bosh, did she say? Ha! I'll give her *bish bash bosh*.

"Yeah?"

"And I'M dumping YOU!" I yell.

"It's Natalie here, actually," says the voice.

"YOU AS WELL!" I thunder.

Two

Getting My Act Together

Mirror, Mirror...

I'M STARING AT MYSELF in the mirror. It's our bathroom mirror, with the shaving light on. It's the least flattering mirror in our house. That's the point. I want to see me looking my worst. I'm "appraising" myself.

Is this the face of an immature, no-fun guy?

I'm too pale.

My hair's too long.

My shoulders are too puny.

I've got no pecs.

Hey—I'm not that bad, though. I'm about how you'd expect me to be at my age. Howza guy supposed to get a more mature look? Without ending up looking like a nerd in a suit and tie or an idiot in a false mustache?

Can't. What we blokes are, that's what we're stuck with, till Nature decides otherwise.

It's different for girls. Girls can transform themselves easier. Dab of makeup here, change of hairdo there; sexy little outfit designed for somebody twice their age. High heels, adding to the height advantage they've already got over us males. Bingo! They're fourteen going on eighteen in thirty minutes. Pubs, clubs, bars—all the rich pickings of adult life within easy reach, if they've a mind.

It's not fair.

While we're at the caterpillar stage, we males oughta lock ourselves away. Do the chrysalis thing in private. Without having girls nagging us to get a move on and telling us how ugly we look. We could burst out of our pupas when we're eighteen. Fit to compete. Masculine credentials at the ready. Self-confidence still intact.

Hmm. Maybe I could up my bish bash bosh rating a bit, though. Have I been been resting on my laurels? Suffering from vacation snooze-button syndrome?

Sandi's accusations have left me gagging for a shot

of extra-strong, high caffeine feel-good factor.

Take my hair. That could definitely do with a makeover. I'll start at the top and hope the feel-good factor filters down rapid fire.

Head First

Mum's back from work. She's lugged in three loaded bags of groceries. I have to rummage through and extract my cereal. I hold it aloft and fire a broadside.

"We ran out."

"So I see," she says, kicking the empty carton on her way to the fridge. She bins it, tight-lipped.

"I suppose you know there was none for my breakfast this morning?"

"So did you go out and get some?"

"What?"

"Go out and get some. You know, from a shop."

"Wha-t? What're you going on about? It's not my job to buy cereal. Buying cereal's your job. You let me run out."

For some reason pointing out this neglect in her nurturing role seems to really annoy my mum. Does she apologize and say she'll not let it happen again? Nah. She jabs her hands on her hips and starts shouting at me.

Apparently it's my fault I've been "lounging around the house all summer," while she's been out "working her socks off." Apparently I'm gonna have to start pulling my weight around here. Then she waves the dirty scrambled-egg pan at me. Shouts that concocting the odd culinary delicacy for myself and leaving the equipment lying around festering's no longer tolerable, either.

Oh, and while we're at it, she's fed up with me going around wearing my ego on the end of my nose, like a boil. I'm going to have to start showing a bit more maturity.

"Maturity." Spot that word popping up again?

Why's everybody forcing me to worry about maturity all of a sudden? Maturity's something you're supposed to grow into. Gradually and painlessly. In your own good time.

Anyway, we're talking two different types here:

- Maturity that impresses girls and other guys
- Maturity that impresses parents

Important I point out the difference.

The first I aspire to; the second, I don't. Who would? So as Mum rants on re maturity type two, I shut my ears. I tip myself a large bowlful of cereal and start munching. There's nothing more calming and comforting than a bowl of cereal, at any time of day. Know those times when you're feeling really hungry? But you don't know what it is you fancy? Take my tip—it's cereal. Never fails.

I wait till Mum's filled the dishwasher, run out of words, and sunk down on a chair with an instant coffee. Then I click the volume back up and raise the other little matter.

"Mum, I need to get my hair cut."

Mum scowls at me. She opens her mouth, then shuts it. "Okay, it is a bit long," she concedes, grudgingly. "You'll find a ten pound note in my purse. Bring me the change."

I groan. "Get real! I can't get it done for a tenner. You're living in the Dark Ages, Mum."

The light of battle ignites in her eyes. "Since when? Sam's Snip Joint's got a special offer on, right now. He's got a sign in the window saying, 'Boys' haircuts £5.50. Limited time only.'"

I sigh. I roll my eyes. "I meant, you know—a trendy haircut. Styled by an expert to suit the shape of my face. That's going to need, er, twenty-five, at least."

Stunned, echoing silence.

A pair of startled eyebrows appear over Mum's coffee mug. "Good grief! Bit young for thinking about spending that amount on your hair, aren't you?"

"Would a girl's mother say that to her?" I snarl. "I think not."

"Oh. . ." Mum puts down her mug. She runs an eye over me.

"This got anything to do with the fact that Sandi's dumped you?"

"Who says she's dumped me!"

"She did. I just met her in town. That nice girl Natalie was with her."

My heart sinks. "Where were they? Proclaiming it outside the town hall? Ringing a hand bell and shouting, 'Oyez! Oyez!'"

"They were by the aromatherapy oils, in Boots."

I cringe at the thought of the three of them discussing *me*, over the aromatherapy oils.

Bet it went like this: "What do they recommend to purge and perk you after off-loading your boring, baby-faced boyfriend?"

"Well, Sandi, this potion composed of ragwort, nettle, and eye of newt looks good."

Why didn't I get my fist in first? Dump her, while I had the chance?

"It was mutual!" I spit. "And if she says otherwise, she's a lying toad. And as for that Natalie—she's a . . . a snake in the grass!" (What does that mean exactly? Not sure, but it sounds treacherous and hissy—and that's Natalie.)

"And what's more, she told me she was bored with town," I fling.

"I'm not taking sides," Mum mutters. "We've known Sandi a long time. You've always been friends.

19

I expect you'll get back together again."

Comforting words. My own opinion exactly. But it's too soon. I'm still smarting and reeling like Sandi socked me in the eye with a three-pound salmon. "Over my dead body! Do you know what she said? She said I'm no fun—in other words, I'm *boring*. She says I've got no bish bash bosh."

That's a smirk Mum's hiding behind her hand.

"I remember telling your dad that," she says.

"Oh? When was that? How old was he?"

"It was last week, I think."

"Great! I've inherited it. I've got boring genes."

Mum gets out her plastic. Flicks the credit card across the table. "Here. Go and get what you need. But I'm not going to make a habit of this. You want to go upmarket again, it comes out of your savings."

"What?"

She shrugs. "The choice is yours. And don't tell your dad. He'd be outraged. When he was your age, your gran sent away for one of those electric hair-clipper thingies. She used to run it over him herself. And you've seen her in action with a lawn mower.

Hmm . . ." she adds, "she's probably still got it, tucked away in a drawer somewhere." (Spot the warning?) "Hadn't you better get a move on? They'll be closing soon."

I put on a pained expression. "I'm not going to Sam's Snip Joint, remember. You have to make an appointment for what I want."

It's all set up. I'm booked at the trendiest salon in town, with a stylist called Baz. Tomorrow morning at 10:15.

My hair's gonna signal to the world: this guy's on the move!

Bad Hair Day

10:15 A.M. Bad start.

The female-person at the reception desk's dead trendy. She's got trendy hair, trendy makeup, trendy black outfit. Pity about her expression, though. She looks like she breakfasted on half a lemon. And the way she's eyeing me outta the corner of her eye you'd think I got my gear courtesy of Oxfam. Great sigh as she's scraping her purple talons down the booking sheet. Am I supposed to apologize for invading her mental space?

Another great sigh as she finds my name's actually there. She reaches for a cape thingie and flips it around my neck. Then she motions me into the waiting section. Thrusts a copy of *GQ* into my hand.

GQ perks me up a bit, actually. It's the current issue. My eyes roam lasciviously over the glamour pics. Airbrushed, of course. Still—wow! I drool over designer clothes I'd sell my soul for. And there's this really engrossing article on spas, "where the fit and well" can get treated with "the care usually dedicated to the chronically sick. . . ."

I'm avidly foddering my daydreams when Baz, my stylist, weaves over. He looks camp. Shaved head, double-pierced eyebrow, bored expression. Still, I trust him. He's an expert. He must be, to work here. Those faintly nicotine-stained fingertips are at the cutting edge of the cutting edge.

"Morning," he yawns, to the top of my head. He tweaks the magazine out of my grasp and leads me across to the "happening" area. Then he starts throwing my hair around with his fingers. Like he's tossing a salad.

I'm sure his expression's changing subtly. Boredom's more like bordering on disdain. Like he's thinking, "Just look at the state of this!" A sort of sinking feeling starts in the pit of my stomach.

"Been here before?" He's frowning. Implying it's obvious I've not? That whoever cut my hair before must've done it with a blunt knife and fork? Or an electric clipper–thingie?

"Er—no," I mutter sheepishly. (Better not mention Sam's Snip Joint.)

My hair's taking on a shape like an atomic explosion. I feel stupid. I look even stupider. No pain, no gain, though. I unclench my hands. I unhunch my shoulders. I try to relax.

"So, what can we do for you, then?" He's fingering his belt that's bristling with surgical-type instruments.

"Er . . . I'm not sure. Can you give me some

advice?" (Ouch. That sounded dead naive. So uncool.)

Baz is frowning. He starts tossing my hair around again. Like he's trying to coax signs of life from it.

"D'you always wash the chlorine out? After you've like, been swimming?"

I glance up at him anxiously through the mirror. What's he getting at? I've been neglecting my hair? It's damaged? Might I actually have let it go beyond repair, only he doesn't want to mention it straight out, 'case I freak? Could it be terminal? A toupee job by the time I'm twenty?

"Er . . . usually," I fib. "Why? Is it a bit out of condition?"

Baz huffs. Then tuts. Then shrugs. "Bit on the dry side," he pronounces.

Not quite terminal yet, then? *Phew!*

"Er . . . what d'you think would suit my face?"

Did he wince? Or have I been reduced to an ultra-sensitive state?

"Prepared to do high maintenance?" he challenges. He flicks a comb through my locks and sweeps them across my forehead, like a nerd's.

"No." I'm sure of myself this time. "L—Low maintenance. Stylish, though . . ." (That's if it's possible. If my hair's not totally beyond his powers of resuscitation.)

"Right. Sounds like a French crop to me. Let's get you washed."

Wow! He *can* do something for me. Relief and gratitude sweep through me.

Thank you! Thank you, Baz!

"Now I'm just going to massage your scalp with this conditioner. So can you try and relax a bit more?" says the trainee-person. How can I when my head's rammed backward over a cruel porcelain washbasin? My neck's gone all stiff and tense. She's already pounded and kneaded my head with shampoo. Now she starts digging into my scalp with her iron-hard fingertips. Can my follicles take it? Baz should have warned her my hair's in a bad way. Needs *gentle* treatment.

"Been anywhere nice on holiday?" she says.

"Er, not especially. I—"

"Oh, right. Back to SCHOOL tomorrow then, is it?"

Great. Even the trainee-person is ageist and despises me. And why when anybody says "school," do they have to go and SHOUT it?

I'm toweled, then abandoned in front of a mirror for a quarter of an hour, staring at my own reflection.

I make an amazing discovery. I've got funny ears. One sticks out, but the other slopes backward. How could I have got to fourteen and never noticed this before? Perhaps it's the way I sleep?

Baz finally reappears. Sprays water over me, like I'm an indoor plant. Then he briskly starts on my locks with the scissors and comb. Snip-snip, snip-snip.

"Been anywhere nice on holiday?" Snip-snip . . .

"Er, no. I—"

"Right. I just flew back from Vegas, day before yesterday. Still jet-lagged. Viva Las Vegas, hey? Ever been to Vegas?"

"Er, no."

"Right. Ever been to the States?"

"Er, no. Not yet. We usually go to Spain or France. Oh, and I've been to Belgium. Once. On Eurostar. I—"

"Right . . ." He yawns.

Snip-snip, snip-snip . . .

He's given up hope of meaningful conversation with me now. Not only do I have hair like an abandoned cornfield, in his estimation I've got no global identity.

He's clicked in to the goings-on in the rest of the salon. The scissors are working on autopilot.

Snip-snip, snip-snip . . .

The shape of my face doesn't seem to be entering the frame. Snip-snip, snip-snip . . .

I expected this expert's whole attention and artistry would be devoted to my personal appearance. That's what I'm paying for, isn't it? Snip-snip.

How can I get his attention back to my precious locks? Snip-snip, snip—while I've still got some left?

Snip.

He's finished!

Already? Is that all the time and attention I get?

He flourishes a hand mirror, so I can see the back view.

Wow. The French go in for their crops really short. I chew my lip. The contours of the back of my head, especially without much hair to soften them, come as a shock.

"Er—it looks, er—great!" I croak.

I'm thinking the opposite. It looks *horrendous*. Don't dare say so, though. I feebly scrape up an expression of bootlicking gratitude instead. I moisten my lips. I inject warmth. I try to deliver the enthusiasm I'm sure Baz feels is due.

"Really, er—GREAT. Er, thanks!"

He whips off my cape. "Right. See you in a two weeks."

Two weeks? At that flipping price?

I needn't have bothered nodding. His head's already swiveled around to pick out his next client.

I crawl over to Ms. Trendy at the desk. Her glance is brief and cold, and her eyes show no reaction as she vanishes my money into the till.

• • •

I emerge through the door reluctantly, feeling like I've been shortchanged.

What I wanted was the dream. The one they tempt you in with, as represented by those blown-up photos of male models in the windows. I wanted the hairdo that combines a personality makeover with a fast-acting maturity agent. That one.

My dream is crushed.

What's walking out of the salon's just the same old *me*. Only with less hair.

Energized!

I steal a furtive glance at myself in a shop window. Like I feared. Baz has turned me into an escapee from Wormwood Scrubs. The convict look might be macho on some, but my bone structure's not noble enough yet to carry it off.

I duck into the shop doorway to get a clearer reflection in the side window.

He's gone and drawn attention to my funny ears. He's made my forehead look like the north face of the Eiger. I look horrendous! All that dosh to get turned into a berk. What'll my mum say?

I step back out onto the pavement. I expose my head to the critical eyes of passersby. Are they looking at me? What are they thinking? Is anybody actually sniggering?

Oh no—guess who just walked past?

My heart's thumping like an overloaded tumble dryer on maximum revs.

Outta all the girl-persons in all the world, fate decrees that Sandi walks past. Just at this very minute. When I'm struggling to come to terms with myself.

She's wearing a new T-shirt with BARBIE IS A TART across the front. In fact, I notice the eye-catching T-shirt before I notice Sandi.

Then she looks at me. Know what? I'll swear that for a split second, she doesn't recognize me. Would you believe that? *Doesn't recognize me*. Then she does, and her mouth drops open.

How do I handle this crisis? I just keep on walking. Don't even turn around.

Wonder what she thought of my hair, though?

I think she looked shocked. . . .

But shocked how? Was it shock as in: shock-horror-what-has-he-gone-and-done-to-himself? Or was it shock that the guy she'd just looked at and failed to recognize was *me*?

Important point, this.

I've a feeling it could've been the second sort. And if it was the second, then I might be right in thinking the first glance she gave me could've had a tinge of "interest" in it. As in: who's that interesting-looking guy I've never noticed around town before?

Hey, how about that?

I stop and give myself a second inspection. In the window of HMV Records.

Different, you've got to admit. I feel a spark of excitement. Perhaps my judgment was too hasty?

Think I'm warming to this hairdo a bit now. Does give me a more streamlined, no-nonsense look, I'll say that for it. What's more, it'll speed up my morning routine no end. No more wetting and gelling, shaking and teasing. There ain't even enough hair left here to pull a comb through.

Plus it'll give me more time for other things. Like . . . doing a few push-ups.

Yeah. How about that? How about raising my fitness level?

It strikes me that bish bash boshness's not just about how you look. Or the state of your mind. It's about your physical well-being, as well.

Bounding energy! *Bish bash bosh*.

I weigh an imaginary badminton racket in my hand.

I thwack an imaginary shuttlecock. Pow-pow! Pow! Pow!

Hey, maybe my new crop has done the trick? Maybe it's unleashed a new, vibrant, sporty-type me?

Thrilling thought.

Can't wait to get back to school tomorrow now. See how all my mates react to the new me.

Show the likes of Sandi Weston that I'm changed on the inside as well as the out.

She's going to be kicking herself for having let me slip through her fingers.

Parental Approaches

"It's—um—yup!" goes Mum, forcing enthusiasm when she sees my hair. "Different. Do *you* like it?"

"Yeah. I do, actually."

"Good."

She flings Dad a challenging look. That look could penetrate armor, but Dad's eyes remain glued to a bill he appears to be sucking horror gratification out of.

"What do you think?" she prompts, using her voice like a cattle prod.

Dad's head jerks up. His eyes swivel from side to side, avoiding any direct confrontation with my head.

"School tomorrow, then," he says.

"Yeah."

"No more dossing around."

"No."

Mum makes a noise like a bus door shutting.

Reluctantly Dad places the bill on the table. He gets up. Starts heading for the back door. But as he passes me, he suddenly rears up on his toes and puts up his fists. Starts pretending to box me.

I parry. I dummy. I duck. I sidestep niftily. Then I head for the fridge.

What we just witnessed was an attempt at male bonding, Dad-style. Under orders from Mum. She must've told him what Sandi said. Decided I need masculine support. Or has she been reading somewhere that strengthening the father/son bond acts as an aid to maturity? Both ways?

Whatever. That was a totally pathetic attempt, Dad.

Know when you're a kid and your ego's been dented? Your dad slips you a quid for a comic or some sweets. Welcome move. When you're a man, I presume he buys you a pint. Ditto. But when you're stuck in the chrysalis stage, what's the best he can come up with?

Punching the space between you.

Doesn't he realize *money* still talks?

Having PPFS (Premature Parental Fatigue

Syndrome) to cope with's bad enough. Now it looks like father/son bonding issues are being raised. Just when I'm already suffering from age deficiency, ego erosion, and end-of-holiday blues.

What a bummer.

I get a carton of orange juice out of the fridge and upend it over a glass.

Nothing comes out but a millimeter of orange sludge.

"And why does nobody in this house even throw away my EMPTY CARTONS ANYMORE?" I holler.

I put it back.

Prominently.

All Ears

6.30 A.M. First morning of a new term of a new school year.

And here I am, out of bed. Ready to start my new fitness regime. No snooze button on *my* alarm anymore!

It'll be twenty minutes on my mum's rowing machine. Quick jog around the block. Cold shower. Healthy breakfast, composed solely of fresh fruit. I think there's an apple left. . . .

But first, I'll kick off with a few warm-up stretches.

Ooomph . . . Not feeling as wide-awake and full of bounce as I'd hoped. Hardly surprising. Over the holidays, I haven't been out of bed before nine most days. My metabolism's got some adjusting to do. Plus I had this really restless night.

My ears are to blame.

Before going to bed, I decided I'd take remedial action. I stuck a large piece of Sellotape across the one that sticks out, training it flat against my head. Behind the other, I put a small wad of cotton, also held in place by Sellotape. Then I attempted to sleep exclusively on my sticking-out-ear side, to aid the flattening process.

Any idea how excruciating it is, trying not to turn over? I developed aches in parts of my anatomy I didn't even know I'd got.

In the end, I gave in.

I surrendered myself to my natural rhythms of sleep. Trusted in the Sellotape to do the job.

Unfortunately, in the middle of the night, the Sellotape from my sticking-out-ear proved not up to coping with the strain. It came unstuck and attached itself with devilish tenacity to my left eyebrow. . . .

Guess I'll just have to live with my ear deformity, until I can afford cosmetic surgery.

"Omygod!" yells Ric, when I get to school. "Who're you out to impress?"

It's the first time he's seen my hair. Great reaction.

He comes charging across the playground and takes a swipe at me with his gym bag.

"Myself," I say, neatly sidestepping. "Numero uno. People like what I do—fine! They don't—tough luck."

I stride away purposefully across the asphalt, looking like I've spotted somebody more interesting to talk to.

I've decided to widen my circle of friends. Stop wasting all my time with losers like Ric. From now on

I intend hanging out with kids who're outstanding for something. Like their brains; sporting achievements; musical or artistic ability; wealthy parents, or—in the case of girls—cracking good looks.

Across the playground I spot Natalie, Sarah, and Becky. They're talking to this girl-on-legs. Not a pair of pins I recognize. But—*phwoar*! They're worth getting to know.

I'm just sashaying over when their owner turns around.

I grind to a halt. Rooted to the spot, like I've just been shot with a stun gun.

It's Sandi.

What does she look like?

What's that she's got dangling from her waist? It's a short school skirt. Where's her usual? Where's that bin-bag-shaped thing that comes down to her ankles?

And what's that on her forehead? A fringe? Sandi's got a smooth, high forehead. I happen to like Sandi's forehead. It makes her look intellectual. I'd persuaded her to grow out her shaggy fringe. Now she's gone and cut one again, only thicker. And she's peering out from underneath it like she's suddenly turned short-sighted.

I know what her game is. Just because I've undergone a big image-change. She's trying to steal my thunder, that's what she's doing.

Hmm . . . interesting reaction, though.

Must mean my own image change struck her as so impressive, she felt she had to compete.

Well, nice try, Sand.

I'm quite flattered, actually.

And great pair of legs. But her usual sports gear—woolly kneesocks, hockey boots, and shorts that look like a female hiker's castoffs—don't do them justice. Whereas black tights zooming out of a scrap of navy serge really does it for me.

Must'nt let on I've noticed, though.

Going into House Assembly, I see Ric again. He's with this quiet, middle-of-the-road kid called Dave. Ric keeps turning around. Shooting me these funny looks. What's he going on about? Can never work out what Ric's expressions mean. They all look like he's just woken up and found himself an orphan, abandoned in the middle of the Sahara Desert.

Suddenly there's a prod in the small of my back.

"Er, excuse me," says this girlie voice.

I turn around. It's Emily, a music prodigy from Year Eight. Emily seems to have been born with a violin case attached to her hand. I've never actually witnessed the instrument under her chin, not being blessed with musical talent myself. But she's got a reputation for being a highly talented scraper of the old catgut.

"Yesss?" I hiss. "What-t?" Letting her know it's a bit inconvenient, having to turn around when assembly's starting. So would she mind spitting out quick why it is she's prodding me?

"Er—um. D'you know you've got a chunk of Sellotape stuck behind your ear?"

I clap a hand to it. The one that slopes backward.

"Oh, that?" I mutter. "Yeah. I do, matter of fact. Thanks, though."

Ooo-oooh. I was living with it before. But now that Emily's reminded me, my right ear starts throbbing like a traction engine.

Assembly's agony.

Straight after I shoot into the loos.

Ever tried peeling a piece of Sellotape off the sensitive area at the back of your ear? When it's been stuck there, bonding with your skin, all night?

I sit smoldering on my own in extended form period. Ric sits with Dave. But at break time he comes over and joins me. Tweaks my ear.

"Got ridda the Sellotape, then? Didn't ya see me giving you them looks, going into assembly?"

"Is that what you were on about? You looked like you were doing an impression of a constipated rooster!"

"Shoulda kept your old hairdo, then nobody'd have known. What's with this new hairdo, anyway? Is it because Sandi's binned you?"

"Let's get this straight," I growl. "It was mutual."

"Yeah," he says dryly. "So I've heard."

"Seen Sandi yet?"

"Yeah. *Phwoar*—fab pair of legs she's been hiding. And what about that new fringe thing, eh?"

I smirk. "If she's trying to grab my attention back,

she's succeeded. But won't let on to her. Not just yet."

Ric gasps and lets out a spluttering sound.

"Not kidding yourself she's got herself up like that to interest *you*, are you? She binned you, man. Wise up."

"We'll see what we shall see," I grind.

"Fringe is what girls use to flirt behind," he chunters. "Mark my words. Be warned."

Why is it you always end up wanting to throttle Ric? Must be a knack he's got.

Why am I wasting break letting a fathead squeeze my anxiety pedal into the floor and dent my ego? When I could have been getting myself a sticky bun?

Year Twelve Two

Double Math period after break, and that's when I run into Sandi again.

She and Natalie are both in my math class. I spot the pair of 'em ahead of me in the scrum on the landing. Natalie gives Sandi a sly dig when she sees me.

Stirring, as usual. Sandi turns and flicks me a look. It's sorta sheepish, I think. Could be she's just having trouble seeing from under the fringe. Or is she using fringe as flirt screen? How do you tell? I give her a nod. No harm in that. And I manage to stop my eyes descending to her legs.

So far, so good.

Then, all of a sudden, Natalie grabs Sandi's arm. Starts pointing out the landing window. My presence gets totally elbowed. Both girls' faces crack into excited grins. Next thing you know, they're jumping up and down. Waving and giggling. Acting really dumb.

By standing on tiptoe and pushing a couple of heads out of the way, I can just manage to see through the window myself.

Two Year Twelve guys are ambling by. That's all.

They can't be the cause of all this girlie excitement. Can they?

Then it all unfolds in slow motion, before my very eyes. Like in a film. . . .

Natalie's banging on the window. The Year Twelve

Two look up and make eye contact. Start grinning back. Then digging each other in the ribs. Then waving back. Just with their fingers, like you do to a baby. Squirmy. I look at Sandi and she's gone all pink in the face. All soppy expression and sparkling eyes. I've seen that look on girls' faces before. At pop concerts.

She never looked at *me* like that.

My mouth goes dry with shock. My stomach churns with disgust. I want to elbow my way through the scrum, grab her, and shake some sense into her. I don't, though. It might look like I care.

$2+1 = 21$

That's what I've just written. Truth is, I'm sitting here in math feeling gutted.

It's that Year Twelve Two.

When Sandi told me she'd started fancying "more mature" guys, I thought she was just saying it. Fantasizing—like you do. Never dawned on me she and Natalie'd already earmarked themselves a real live pair. From our own school. That she'd be putting on a mating display under my very nose. With the eyes of half the school on her—and me.

That's a big difference between girls and us. We males are happy just fantasizing. Girls, they have to go and make it happen.

It's really humiliating.

I blame Natalie.

It's not even as if those guys are sex gods.

Believe me—they're dead ordinary.

One's got these long, spindly legs that put me in mind of a stick insect. The other's got this totally dire haircut. That's really hard to stomach. Seriously—he looks like he got barbered at Sam's Snip Joint. Sandi dumped *me* so she could go after *them*? She cut a fringe and put on a short skirt to attract *them*?

Why?

They've got zilch going for them.

Apart from their age. Year Twelve.

"My boyfriend, who's in the Sixth Form . . ."

How d'you compete with that?

Deep, exasperated sigh unexpectedly escapes me, like a fart.

• • •

Picture a motorcar with all the air let out of its tires and a potato stuffed up its exhaust. I'm the human equivalent. I can rev my engine and blast my horn as hard as I like. Sandi-wise, I ain't going nowhere.

Not unless I can perform miracles.

Age myself by a couple of years.

If only.

Sixteen: the male springboard to all the pleasures of adult life. Year Ten girls are dancing flamenco, performing wheelies, pulling rabbits out of hats, and jumping through fiery hoops—anything, just to grab your attention. Even if you're boring, ugly, and got about as much sex appeal as a hibernating tortoise!!!

Urrgh . . .

I definitely blame Natalie. Sandi used to have more sense.

I feel tired suddenly. Really knackered. I smother a yawn.

Hardly surprising, after forcing myself out of bed at 6:30 A.M., on little sleep. Then subjecting my body to all that unaccustomed physical exercise.

My head starts to nod.

I'm starving as well. A Granny Smith and the remains of an overripe banana are all very well. But they're not as filling as a bowl of Coco Pops and a strangled egg on toast. I didn't even get a sticky bun at break.

Now my stomach's started complaining. I clench it.

The second period of math is torture.

I'm trying to stop my stomach rumbling, prop my eyelids open, stop myself yawning, and keep my head from nodding. My ear's still stinging. My ego feels like it's been mugged.

I wanna go home. I wanna scrub out this morning. I wanna start again, on a clean board . . .

I get a mobile text message.

"u luk lyk a cocont. Sand."

Three

Sporting Chance

Role Model

AMAZING HOW A BLOB of Savlon, some good nosh, a lounge in front of the telly, and a decent night's sleep revives you.

At school yesterday I hit rock bottom. If somebody'd thrown me a spade, I could've reached Australia.

But as from now, I'm bouncing back.

I've got my pride to consider.

No female duo—one who's obviously in the throes of some hormonal crisis, the other who's into emotional terrorism—gets to decide *my* destiny.

Bet I've got more bish bash bosh potential in me than that Year Twelve Two spliced and duplicated a dozen times over. And now I'm even more determined to tap into it. Then *whooshhh*! Sandi Weston and Natalie Redfern, you'd better duck, or you might get flattened by the blast.

Only I'm pacing myself more carefully from now on. This morning I slept till 7:30. Then I limited myself to only half a dozen push-ups. And I ate a bowl of cereal and an egg on toast. I was pushing myself too hard, too fast before. You can't turn your body into a finely tuned precision instrument in twenty-four hours. You need patience.

I'm just arriving at our school gates when I see this guy Gary Grant being chauffeured by his mum. They pull up right outside. Not discreetly around the corner, where the rest of us get dropped off.

Gary Grant's only in my year. But somehow *he* seems to have got wired up to his bish bash bosh factor already. Gary walks the walk, talks the talk.

I watch him, striding outta the car like he's up for it. Confident angle to his chin; casual, unfazed expression in his eyes. Whatever a school day lobs at Gary, you reckon he can cope.

What's this? His mum's fussing outta the car as well. He's letting her?

She's heading for the boot. Ah. Going to unload his

gear. Not in the role of Mum. More in the role of porter, valet, or other-type servant. That's okay, then.

First Gary's mum hauls out his school bag. Hands it to him.

Now she's struggling with his sports bag. This is *big*. It's a *Head Holdall 2000*, and it's stuffed to the gills. This is seriously *heavy*. As in sack of coal or prize pig.

Can Gary's mum lift it?

Gary stands rolling his eyes and sighing as she goes for the third attempt.

She's buckling at the knees, staggering a bit . . .

Hey—she's done it!

She looks up at Gary for approval, but I see she gets none. Old Big Head's tapping his foot and eyeing his watch.

Now Gary's mum's going for his second sports bag. This one's lighter. A backpack. Must contain his recreational sports gear, because I can see the handle of his badminton racket sticking out. Gary's mum has less of a struggle here. She installs this one over his shoulders.

"Is that all, Gary?" I hear her asking. She's cranking

her back straight again and eyeing him like an anxious spaniel.

He thinks for a second. Then clicks his fingers. "Dosh!" he says, accusingly.

"Oh, sorry, Gary!"

His mum scuttles around the car to get her handbag. Extracts what looks like a tenner from her purse and hands it over.

"Is that enough?"

"Do for now."

"Oh, good!" She's beaming with relief. Like he's just paid her a compliment. "Well, have a good day . . ."

But she says that to Gary's back. He's already strode off.

I follow Gary as he progresses across the playground.

Here and there he bestows a curt nod. You expect the kids to shoot to attention and salute.

Halfway across, he's accosted by Lyndsey. Lyndsey's a total babe. To die for. But I notice Gary hardly changes his stride. And when he turns to speak to her, he nearly decapitates her with the handle of his bad-minton racket. Lyndsey ducks. Instead of bawling him out, like you'd expect, she just giggles, like it's gynormously funny.

Does Gary apologize? Nah. I even hear him telling her he has to go off-load his stuff, so she'll have to catch him later.

How cool can you get?

Hmmm . . .

Very interesting, all this . . .

Not to Be Sniffed At

From observing Gary, I think I might have located two important factors that are preventing me from achieving the inner security and well-being that result in bish bash bosh.

• My parents' failure to give me their contin-uing and concentrated support (PPFS).
• I'm not sporty enough.

Re factor one: take this morning, for instance. It seems I just happened to tip all the remains of the milk over my bowl of Coco Pops. Leaving none for my mum's coffee.

How would Gary Grant's mum react under these circumstances?

She'd probably smile indulgently. Say, nurturingly, "Well, my son's a growing boy and needs his calcium . . ."

How does *my* mum react?

She thwacks at me with last night's copy of the *Evening Post*. And what she actually says, I'm not gonna repeat. But the gist of it is that I'm a selfish and greedy pig and should feel bad about myself.

Spot the difference?

I leave the house feeling bad. Lugging a tacky old sports bag from last season. On foot and under-funded.

My parents are obviously failing me and have got a lot to answer for.

Re factor two: my lack of sporting achievement. Well, I'm above average height and weight for my age. I've got full use of my faculties. All my limbs are in sound working order. So why've I never been picked for a school team? Answer me that.

Could it be 'cause the PE staff hate me?

Or could it be 'cause I've just not been putting in the effort?

Okay, it's the second. I admit it.

Sports-wise, it ain't nobody's fault but my own.

It's all up to me. If I want to do well, I've got to psyche myself up.

With the right mental attitude, who knows? School team today . . . Olympic team tomorrow.

Why not?

Aim high, that's my motto.

Hmmm . . . my mum did refuse to buy me that high-protein muscle-power supplement in strawberry flavor when I asked her for it, though. That could have made a difference. And then there's the little matter of that heart-rate monitor watch, with calendar and daily alarm, water-resistant to fifty feet and a bargain at £49.99 that I wanted, but Dad vetoed. . . .

But I've gotta put all that behind me.

First Games lesson of the new school year's coming up this afternoon.

My chance to show what I can really do on the sports field. My chance to get picked for the Year Ten Rugby Team. Release my sporting bish bash bosh!

Only first I'll have to overcome my changing-roomitis.

I always get this really bad attack at the start of term. The cleaners have been in over the holidays. Instructed to do a "thorough" operation. They just make things worse. They round up all the usual suspects: cheesy socks; festering garments; stiff, stinky towels; and putrid footwear. They secure them in bin bags, to be known henceforth as "Lost Property" and opened only at your peril. Then they dutifully scrub and disinfect everything in sight, while ignoring everything that's not.

Useless!

They could seal off the whole place in plastic wrap and marinate it in Yves Saint Laurent pour Homme for six weeks. It'd still do no good.

The smell's so deeply ingrained, only a fire could

destroy it. Take rancid sweat, a dollop of mud, a dash of stale water, and a lingering blast of Deep Heat. Throw in disinfectant and start-of-term turmoil of hormones, and you've got a brew that sets my stomach churning like the wheel of a paddle steamer.

Urrrrrgh . . .

Why doesn't somebody invent nose filters? Seriously—could make a fortune!

However, dragging my mind back from its entrepreneurial ramblings . . .

I've not only got to fight and conquer this weakness, I've got to learn to love the smell. I've got to learn to stand on the threshold, tanking myself up on great gulps of it, like Gary Grant. Or, if I can't manage this, I've got to find some way to turn my phobia to my advantage. Use it as a key to unlock my pent-up adrenaline.

Let's face it, I've gotta do something if I want to make my mark. Faintness and stomach cramps don't create the right mental attitude for sporting prowess. Especially on the rugby pitch.

Up for It

"Aw—no!" squeaks Ric. He's squirmed himself into a space next to mine to get changed. "I don't believe it!"

He's standing with his school trousers dangling over his arm, staring down at his undercarriage.

"What?" Better ask and get it over with. Knowing Ric, he'll tell me anyway.

"I forgot it was Games when I got dressed. Went and put my boxers on!"

"Ooops," I smirk. "No flying tackles for you this afternoon then, my son. Not unless you want to display your flying tackle."

I deliberately raise my voice as I deliver this quip. My clever pun's too good to waste on Ric. I'm rewarded with a few sniggers from last season's squad, who I just happen to be changing opposite.

My joke's being repeated and passed around. Very satisfactory. Ups my feel-good factor several notches.

Ric pretends to laugh.

In spite of his need to stay out of the action even more than usual—if that's humanly possible—guess what he's doing now? He's smearing his legs with Vaseline, just in case. If he can't avoid making contact with the ball, tackling him'll be like grappling with a halibut.

"Here," I mutter, "give me some of that, will you?"

"Get yer own! This cost 99p at Superdrug."

"Mean sod!"

Right. Here I am, then, jogging out on to the pitch and limbering up. I'm feeling not so bad, so far. Pity my legs didn't see any sun this summer. Still, look on the bright side—they're not as white as Ric's. His have got all the slitheriness and general qualities of a couple of strands of cooked spaghetti.

Mr. Hardcastle, our Games teacher (known as Hardy) is sorting us into teams.

I'm a back. Fine.

I take up my position.

Head up! Chest out!

Think bish bash bosh! Think brave! Think bold! Think—HAKA!

•　•　•

I'm knackered. Sagging. It's really difficult keeping the up-and-at-'em body language alive when your performance is less than mediocre.

My mind's starting to wander . . .

Strewth! Somebody just passed to Edward. Must've been a mistake. Nobody ever passes to Edward deliberately. Edward's so shocked himself, he drops the ball like it's a hot potato. Which gives Kenzo Kurimoto the chance to grab it.

Oh no—Kenzo's thundering down my side of the pitch at a speed of approximately a hundred miles per hour! He's built like a tank, this boy. When Kenzo's on a charge, he's unstoppable.

No. *Not* unstoppable! Think positive. Think *tackle*.

"Tackle him, you great berk!" somebody yells, echoing my own thoughts.

But . . . arrgh! Kenzo's got these legs as thick as railway sleepers. With size-ten boots attached. Great big muddy boots with great big plastic studs sticking out. Studs that could smash your teeth down the back of your throat with twice the force of a knuckle-duster.

But if I want to make my mark, I've gotta stop him.

So stop quivering and go fer it! Go fer glory! Go fer gold! Think Saint George and England. Twickenham throbbing to the strains of "Swing Low, Sweet Chariot."

I uproot myself from the spot. I spring after him. I fling myself sideways. I grab the human tank around his great thighs. I cling on to them, eyes shut, like a drowning man.

There's a thud and a couple of winded gasps as we both hit the ground. The ball bounces out of his grasp and into touch.

I've felled him. Kenzo Kurimoto!

Wow!

Me.

I'm dazed. Amazed. So savoring the moment, I forget to let go. Kenzo's threshing in my grasp. He's elbowing me and shouting, "Gerroff—psycho!"

Now everybody's congratulating me on my magnificent tackle. Gary Grant, my games teacher, everybody. Except Kenzo. He seems to be taking it all a bit personally.

"Good God!" hisses Ric. "Got the death wish? Is that what having a ballsy haircut does for you?"

Wow!

The adrenaline's really pumping now. My ego's twice the size of David Beckham's annual earnings.

Double wow!

Bet this beats sex!

Mixed Reactions

"So I'm on the rugby team," I say to Ric in what's known as a stage whisper. We're walking out of school and just happen to be passing Sandi and Natalie.

Ric groans. Gives me a dig.

"If that's meant to impress who I think it is," he mutters, "you're wasting your time."

"What?"

He waits till we're safely out of earshot of the cackling duo.

"Know those guys in Year Twelve they've got their sights on?"

"Yeah. So?"

"School First Fifteen. Pair of 'em."

I swallow. "So?" I repeat.

Ric shrugs.

"Can't stand me getting a bit of success, can you?" I snarl. "Gotta try and spoil it."

"Just a friendly warning," he says.

I've scraped the skin off my elbow. Funny how you don't notice pain in the heat of success.

Skin off my elbow, skin off my ear.

Tapping into my bish bash bosh ain't half taking its toll on my physical well-being.

Gotta get toughened up, though.

Okay, I'll admit it. Ric's revelation's taken some of the shine off my sporting ambitions. But I've gone and fully committed myself now.

"Mom," I say, when she gets in from work. "Guess what? I tackled this big kid in rugby today. Felled him like a tree! Been picked for the team on Saturday."

My mum's smile fades. "Oh, er, well done," she says, grudgingly. Then a frown appears. "Not turning into one of those great macho-hairy-brutes, are you?"

She might at least try to look pleased. Gary Grant's mum would've pinned a medal on him.

"You've got a really negative attitude toward me," I glower. "Know that? You never give me any praise for anything."

She groans. "I said well done. What more do you want me to do? Pin a medal on you?"

Typical.

My dad's reaction's a different kettle of fish, though.

When Mum tells him the news, guess what he does?

He actually eyeballs me. Without the worried frown. Without the puzzled, "which planet did this thing come from?" expression. Instead, a smile breaks out. I find myself basking in the forgotten warmth of . . . recognition!

Start up the mood music, roll the drums. Pump up the technicolor! I am no longer an insoluable mathematical equation—I AM HIS SON.

He gives me a high five. Then jumps up and down, punching his fists in the air. As excited as if the Lions had just slaughtered the Wallabies 40-0. Says he's coming to give me sideline support on Saturday. Starts getting out ancient photos of himself on school teams. And going into shuddering detail about his twice-broken collarbone. Insisting I examine the deformity he carries to this day.

Oh heck! What button have I accidentally pressed here?

Is he seeing rugby as something that'll bridge the gap? The yawning chasm that lies between taking me to the park to play on the swings and taking me down to the pub for a pint?

Have my efforts to increase my bish bash bosh inadvertently hit on what Dad sees as the male-bonding, Dad-as-role-model opportunity Mum's been at him to find?

I catch a man-to-man flash of zeal in my father's eyes, and my innards shrink.

It's not how you think it is, Dad.

This is not gonna happen.

I'm a fake.

Over and Out

Good news is, Dad's persuaded Mum to agree to me having a new white rugby shirt, plus a pair of Lycra undershorts. Good for morale. At least I'll feel confident I'm looking good and nothing's in danger of hanging out. Oh, yeah. I've got some Deep Heat and a tub of Vaseline as well.

Bad news is, I've just heard we're playing Udderstone. Or, as they're commonly known in rugby circles, the Breaker's Yard Boys.

There was a queue at Casualty last time we played them, according to Gary Grant.

Even worse news: Dad's gone and canceled a Saturday morning appointment, just to watch me play.

Worser than worse news: Dad's taken his tracksuit out of mothballs and intends to wear it.

Omygod! This Saturday is turning into the *worst* day of my life. Why did I pick *sports* to get involved in?

First I turn up to find we're not playing in our *white* shirts. Turn's out white's our *away* uniform. We're playing in blue. Only I haven't brought my blue. All I've got's my smart, Daz-white, brand-new white.

Well, nobody told *me*.

Hardy's unsympathetic comments don't do much for my level of morale. Then he sinks it even further. He orders me to search out a blue top from: *Lost Property*.

I unearth one.

Urrgh—it stinks!

Urrgh—it's VAST! Drop me out of an airplane and I'd not be needing a parachute.

And now I've seen the Udderstone coach arriving.

They're all six feet tall and built like Kenzo (only slight exaggeration here—they're *tough*. Believe me, they're bone-crushingly tough).

And my dad's here. Wearing the tracksuit and showing off. Going everywhere on the jog and bouncing on his toes and sticking his chest out. Trying to make out he's a fitness instructor or in training for the London Marathon.

And Sandi's here. With Natalie. But not to support *us*, their own year. Oh no! They're here to support their lover boys in the First XV. Well good, says I. Would I *really* want Sandi watching me? Especially when I'm decked out in a shirt that looks like it's been designed for a gorilla. And smells like a gorilla's been in it. (What *is* that stink? *Phaugh!*) Pity, though. I'd love to ask her if she's brought her silver pom-pom-thingies and her ra-ra skirt.

Hardy's calling me over. What for?

"Denis has turned up," he says, pointing at Den.

I nod at Den. So what? I'm thinking.

"I've been off with food poisoning," says Den.

"But he says he's okay now. Fit to play," says Hardy. "So you're on the bench, lad. Right?"

Thud! His words hit me smack in the solar plexus.

"Yeah. R-Right," I stutter. "Right."

Off the field before I've even been on!

Relegated. Just like that.

Can he do that? Is it legal? Is it *sporting*? Is it *National Curriculum*?

But suddenly there are all these complicated emotions fighting each other for control of my brain.

Relief—I'll not have to face the Breaker's Yard Boys. Yeah!

Shame—I'm being substituted by the likes of *Den,* who's half a foot shorter than me and whose nickname is "Gerbil."

Anxiety grabs me and puts me in an armlock. How the heck am I going to break this humiliating news to my dad? At this very minute, he's out there on the pitch, hobnobbing with the other sporty dads. Cementing his credibility. He's *proud* of me for once. He's going to be so unforgivingly gutted when he hears this news, I might have to take up residence in our garden shed.

And I've all this mental angst to cope with, while I'm wearing a shirt that's not mine. A shirt that's got sleeves that keep sliding down and dangling over my hands. A shirt that, underneath the overpowering odor of gorilla, has got this other peculiar pong . . .

I sniff the front. I sniff the armpits. Urrgh—stale, rose-scented deodorant.

I'm plumbing the depths of humiliation here.

I wanna disappear.

I'm definitely gonna play the cowardly card and steer well clear of my dad.

Why didn't I go? Just *go*? Anywhere.

If I'd bunked off, I wouldn't have just got called onto the field. As Gary Grant's blood replacement. When we're in desperate straits. When we're losing 31-0. Even though so many of their players have been sin-binned for really unsavory incidents and they must've played nearly half the match with only fourteen men.

At least nobody can accuse *me* of losing us the match.

There's this really chilly silence from the touchline as I trot on. Being beaten's bad enough, but being slaughtered, well, that's like . . . really *uncomfortable*.

I risk eye contact with my dad. He must be dead relieved I'm on, but he doesn't show it. He looks all keyed up. Nervous I'm gonna disgrace him. But I bet he's secretly hoping for a miracle. Hoping I might, just might, bring some honor to the family name. Reestablish his now shrinking credibility as sporty dad.

Oh no—there's Sandi! What's she doing, slumming on our touchline? She's got this really pained expression on her face. Don't blame her. The First XV match has already ended. They must've had a famous victory, judging by all the cheering.

And suddenly *I'm* being thrust on, with my sleeves dangling over my hands and my shirt dangling down over my knees. How'm I supposed to exude confidence and bish bash bosh looking like this? I try tucking the folds of my shirt into my shorts. But my shorts just ain't got the spare capacity. I try rolling my sleeves up above my elbows then jamming my elbows into my sides. I try to pretend I'm the secret, last-resort weapon. Rather than just the last resort.

Right. Here we go. . . .

Keep moving. Don't let the mask of enthusiasm slip. Keep out of trouble. That's the plan. It actually works, for a bit.

But suddenly there's these excited shouts, because somebody's got the ball to Kenzo and he's started on what turns out to be this amazing fifty-yard run down the left wing.

"Go on, Kenz! Gofer it!" I'm yelling. And I set off in excited support.

He ploughs his way through one tackle; shrugs off another. But there's a whole posse of Breaker's Boys closing him down. He's gonna have to pass back . . . gonna have to . . .

I can see him glancing around. Do the same myself.

Then a look of despair shadows both our faces. The Breaker's Boys are closing in for the kill and we know he's got no alternative. He's going to have to pass to . . . *me*.

My fresh legs have outstripped everybody else's.

No time to think. With the shouts of our supporters ringing in my ears (is that Dad's voice shouting, "Move your ass! Move your ass!") I swing into action.

But as soon as my arms swing into motion, guess what? My sleeves flop down.

Kenzo flings the ball in my direction and—nightmare scenario—I've got *no hands*!

I fling out my arms, like a performing seal, catching the ball in my flippers. Oooopsadaisy!

Fate's with me, for once. Somehow I manage to control the slithery egg shape. I cradle it to my chest with my left arm and set off in a sort of waddling sprint for the goal line, trying to disentangle my right hand as I go. Can hear feet pounding behind me. Feel breath panting down my neck. Hands snatching at the folds of my shirt.

I'm never gonna make it . . .

Not gonna make it . . .

Never expected to MAKE IT.

I shake my right hand free to ground the ball— *Ooouuuumph*.

But I'm over!

SCORED!

A sensational try, right between the posts.

Our *only* try.

I scrape myself up from the mud to a crescendo of cheers.

This is the pinnacle of my sporting career.

My fifteen minutes of fame as a sporting hero.

I'm in pain, though.

I watch as Gareth converts. But under the mud and strained, heroic smile, I know I'm staggering around as white as a sheet. Praying for the whistle to go off.

I heard this crack as I went down, with a two-hundred-pound body on top of me. And I'm trying not to faint.

Yeah, it's official. I paid for my success. I fell victim to the Breaker's Yard Boys.

Broken collarbone. Arm in a sling. I blame my dad.

Well, if he broke his collarbone *twice*, I reckon it's more than just bad luck. I reckon there could be some congenital weakness there. I tell him so.

Thanks a bundle, Dad!

But my dad disclaims the blame. I'd not done a proper preseason build-up, he says. Nor was I properly mentally prepared, he says. And I was unfairly encumbered by my shirt. Now, if only he'd known I was going to start taking an interest in rugby, at last, he could have taken my coaching personally in hand.

"Yeah," I mutter, pretending to look really miffed. "Yeah." But what I'm secretly thinking is, *Yeah!*

Guess what? It'll take *weeks* for my collarbone to heal. And after that, it could take even more time to get the rest of my body fit again. If I play my cards right, I might manage to not be called on to play for . . . the whole flipping season!

So while my dad's smarting over lost opportunities, I'm thinking, better to quit my sporting career while I'm on top, because there must be easier ways of acquiring bish bash bosh than on the rugby pitch. Gotta be.

Sorry your dreams have been shattered though, Dad.

At least I didn't totally disgrace you, did I?

You should be thankful for small mercies.

I know *I* am.

Four

In Demand

Touché

AT SCHOOL ON MONDAY, Sandi comes over. Speaks to me. It's the first time since our breakup.

"Saw your try," she says, attempting to blow the fringe out of her eyes.

"Really?" I say, playing it cool. "Wonder you could see anything, under that hedge."

"Jonny Wilkinson needn't feel threatened."

"Listen." I jut out my chin in a passable imitation of an actor in a World War II movie who's lost a limb and been awarded the Victoria Cross for bravery. "I'll be the first to admit I'm not your typical big, hairy rugby player. I was just a conscript, doing my duty. Battling for the sake of the school."

Sandi makes this huffing, puffing noise.

I glower at her. "And Florence Nightingale needn't feel threatened."

"Idiot!" she groans. "Florence Nightingale's been stripped of her female-carer-icon status. She's been proved to be just an interfering, bullying old bag."

"Ah, right. In that case, I take it back. She should feel threatened."

"Oh *you*," she hisses. "I was going to say sorry about your arm. Only now I'm not!"

And she stalks off, short skirt swinging.

"It's my clavicle!" I yell after her. "At least get the anatomy right!"

Think I can chalk up that little skirmish as a victory to me, don't you? It's not exactly the sorta scene I had in mind, though.

Sandi stalking off, looking like a cat that's been offered yesterday's leftovers, ain't the groveling cat-outside-the-window-on-a-wet-and-stormy-night I'd have liked. But Sandi's always had a tongue that could rasp the bark off a tree.

A sling definitely ups my profile. Marks me out as a shaker, if not a mover. It's dead obvious she couldn't resist my wounded hero appeal. She's just not admitting it to herself, yet.

Musical Interlude

"Tough luck about your arm," says this girlie voice. It's lunch break and I'm trying to cope, one-handed, in the lunch queue. It's Emily, the music prodigy. Seems even little Year Eight girl-persons want to commiserate. Pity Sandi Weston's not still around to witness this.

"Collarbone, actually," I point out.

"Oh, right."

I glance at Emily out of the corner of my eye. It occurs to me that she must know a thing or two about one-handedness herself, her left hand having a violin case permanently attached.

I watch her skillfully maneuvering her tray one-handed. Delicately loading it with an egg salad platter, an apple, and a glass of orange juice. She's coping really well.

I decide to compliment her on her skills in the one-handed department. When I do, she laughs, like I've said something dead witty.

This is the second time Emily's seized the opportunity to strike up a conversation. Wonder if she fancies me?

Emily's quite pretty, actually. In a twelve-year-old sort of way. Clever as well. And reputed to be a really talented musician.

I'm quite flattered by her attentions. This is more like it.

We neither of us fancy carrying our trays one-handed very far. So it seems okay if we both plonk them down together at the nearest table.

Emily detaches the violin case and places it on a vacant chair. Then know what she does? She offers to cut my toad-in-the-hole into bite-size pieces. Even though she herself's a vegetarian. How about that?

She's a nice little girl, Emily. She's got this soft, gentle voice. You can't imagine yourself trading insults with her. I bet you'd never hear her shrieking and being raucous. Or see her wiggling her butt in a short skirt, like some I could name. Emily's skirt comes just below her knees. And her shoes are sensible and polished.

"I hear you play that thing really well," I say, nodding at the violin case. Showing I can make conversation on artistic matters.

"Haven't you ever heard me?"

"Er, er . . . well . . . no," I confess, having to let on that I've never turned up at a school concert. "I'd like to hear you sometime, though."

"Have you got a favorite piece for the violin?" she asks.

Wow, in-depth stuff! "Er, not really . . ." I start searching my brain. Surely I can come up with *something*? What tunes does that bloke perform who plays the fiddle and supports Aston Villa team soccer? What about Bond? Yeah. What *about* Bond?

I'm sure my brain's on the point of going ping. I've got my fingers all ready to click. Then I spot Ric in the lunch queue. Oh no! The sighting throws me right off. Bet he'll come charging over and butt in. Start creating waves in this gentle sea of polite, arty conversation Emily and I are carefully navigating.

He does.

Ric clatters his tray down on our table. He grabs Emily's violin case, showing it no reverence whatsoever, and dumps it on the floor. Then he parks his bum and grins at me. Relief is at hand, me old mate, he's signaling. He cocks his eye in Emily's direction and puffs out his cheeks, as in "Year Eight female nerd." It'd never occur to him I might *want* to talk to her.

I shoot him a frown, but it slides off.

Now he's spotted Emily's talented little hands in the act of slicing up my sausage. I catch a glint in his slitty little eyes. Oh no—he wouldn't, would he?

The warning kick I aim at Ric gets deflected off the table leg. It slops Emily's orange juice. But Ric doesn't even brake. Once this kid's got his brain in gear, there's no stopping him.

"Ou-uch," he sets off, with an ugly leer. I cringe. I'm so cringed-up, I hardly register his pathetic sausage crudity.

Ric chortles a dirty chortle at his own pathetic

humor. He's the only one that does.

You've got to hand it to Emily. She just gives him this cool, blank stare. Then she shoves my plate back to me and starts on her salad.

"D'you sing?" she asks me in her crisp little voice. "Mr. Davis is short of boys for the choir."

"Er . . . Well, I was in the choir at my first school. Only—"

"His voice has broken," Ric grunts through a mouthful of batter. "Should hear him! Sounds like an old tom cat with tonsilitis. A police siren's got more music in it. Ever tried rubbing a pair of rusty tin cans together?"

"I was even picked to do a solo one Christmas," I continue, ignoring him. "'Wind Through the Olive Trees.'"

Ric splutters.

I groan. Pathetic!

Ric starts to guffaw. He guffaws so much, he starts to choke. He's choking so hard, I have to thump him on the back. I thump him *hard*.

Emily stares down at her plate and selects a slice

of egg. Disassociating herself.

Ric resurfaces and wipes the tears of laughter from his eyes. "Hey—remember that Elvis the Pelvis karaoke video somebody lent you once?" He gurgles. "Nearly drove your mum up the wall, didn't ya?" He spears his own sausage and starts pretending it's a mike. "You ain't nothin' but a hound dog . . ." he growls.

Why didn't I thump him *harder* while I had the chance?

Emily seems to have reached a decision. She polishes off her orange juice and picks up her apple. "I have to dash, now," she says, under his gyrating arm. "Got a rehearsal for the school concert in the music room. You could come and hear me, if you like. When you've finished your lunch." She throws a look in Ric's direction. It plainly says, "Only don't bring your pet moron."

"You haven't finished your salad," I say, guiltily. "You've hardly touched it."

All she's consumed is a couple of lettuce leaves and a slice of egg.

"I've had enough," she says meaningfully.

"Hey, can I finish it off, then?" Ric says. Has he no shame?

Emily thrusts it at him. She mouths "See ya" at me. Then she gathers up her instrument and goes. While her dignity's still intact. Don't blame her.

"Soon got rid of her, didn' I?" Ric boasts. He slides her salad on top of his toad-in-the-hole that's swimming with onion gravy. "Somebody oughta tell that Emily where to stick that violin case of hers, eh?" he grunts. "Looks like she's already swallowed the bow."

"Here," I say. I tip the remains of my lunch on top of the salad. His plate resembles a compost heap. "Stuff that in yer mouth as well. It'll keep it occupied."

"Hey, what's bitten you? Don't tell me you *fancy* little Emily?" he gasps, forking the gravy through.

I groan. "No, I don't. Some of us haven't got girls on the brain."

"Since when? What's gotten into you?"

"Nothing. Forgeddit."

I get up and wander off.

Ego Tripped Up

I'm dead certain Emily fancies me. But I've no intention of letting on to Ric. No way. Might as well paint a target on my backside and hand him a crossbow with a permit to shoot.

Hmm . . . Can't help smirking to myself. If girls your own age are chasing older boys, stands to reason some of the younger girls must be fancying *you*. Cheering thought. Why didn't I click on to it before? Not that I'm into fancying younger girls yet. But I've no objection to being admired by them, from afar.

I'm quite tempted by Emily's invitation to hear her practicing. Thing is, I wouldn't mind having a shot at mixing with the musicians. They're the stuck-up elite at our school. Well, they think they are. They walk around school looking like they're going somewhere. And they get to spend not only break but lunchtime as well in the music room, if they like. Bonding with each other. 'Stead of having to survive outside in the jungle, like the rest of us.

Pity I've got no musical talent of my own, though. If my mum and dad had *forced* me to play an instrument, I might have developed some. Only they didn't. All they ever got me was a set of bongo drums. And even that got sabotaged after a week. I still suspect my dad.

Think I will just pop to the music room and show my face. Check out the possibilities—if any—of the musical social scene. Nothing to lose.

I'm just moseying over in the direction of the music block, when I spot Emily. She's trotting along ahead of me, making a bee line. Violin case in one hand, big red apple in the other. I smile to myself. At least you know where you stand with a girl like Emily. I put on a spurt to catch up with her.

Hey. What's she up to? She's changing direction! Making a detour across the lawn. She's heading toward a Year Twelve guy.

I grind to a halt.

It's *him*. The Year Twelve twerp with the stick-insect legs!

Emily goes straight up and accosts him. She's standing up on tiptoe, saying something to him. He's stooping down, listening. Laughing. Now she's holding up her apple—offering him a bite! He chews off half the flipping apple before he hands it back. Then he tweaks her hair and wanders off in the direction of the dining hall.

My eyes are popping out on stalks, I can tell you.

I'm talking seriously *stunned* here.

Emily?

Innocent little Emily, from Year Eight? With her sensible skirt and her polished shoes and her cool I-am-above-the-common-herd facial expressions? Emily's at it as well? Chasing after the Sixth Form!

I feel like I've just witnessed Little Red Riding Hood snogging the Big Bad Wolf, in full view of Grandma.

And he was *responding*. Taking whacking great bites out of her apple. When only the other day he was doing smarmy waving at Sandi.

I slink away, in the opposite direction to the music room. Choking on the bitter pill of truth.

Groupie material—that's all Emily saw me as.

Hanger-on status—that's all I'd have had in the music room. A doer of odd jobs that are beneath me. A putter-out of music stands.

My bish bash bosh's hit a bum note.

My self-confidence needle's plummeted to zero.

My ego feels like it's shot from penthouse to basement in ten seconds flat.

Can't even cut the mustard with Year Eight!

Five

Partying with the A-list

Stratford or Bust

CRISIS!

We're supposed to be paying for the Stratford trip in English, first lesson. It's form period and somebody's just reminded me. Pay up today, Ms. Jackson warned, or you're not on board.

But I've got no signed parental consent form. No check. No astronomic amount of cash about my person. Not like Gary Grant, who's currently forging his dad's signature and meeting the emergency out of dosh from his inside blazer pocket, plus a loan from Lyndsey.

Ric's got his. Form and check are sealed in a smug cream envelope with his mum's bold, efficient hand-writing on the front.

Where's mine?

I told my mum. Waved the form under her nose. In the kitchen. Days ago.

So where is it now?

Heaven knows.

Folded into a wedge for steadying the table? Submerged under a pile of bank and Powergen statements? Binned in a ruthless drive to clear the kitchen work surfaces of junk mail?

Why did my mum not pin it on the kitchen notice board, like she used to? Why did she not talk about the trip, raising my levels of excitement, expectation, and focus, like she used to? Why was the form not eventually sealed in an envelope with a check, like Ric's, and placed in my school bag?

She forgot, that's why.

Lost interest in her son's affairs, that's why.

And she'll shrug off the blame if I have to stay behind at school while the rest get bussed off to Stratford. Claim it's my own fault. Show no remorse that I've missed seeing a major production of our Shakespeare exam text. Rendering me unable to answer questions on production, lighting, sound effects, and set. Thereby causing me to fail exam, get bad reports, and end up a lavatory attendant.

It's terrifying to think how PPFS could blight my life, shriveling my youthful, expectant shoots through lack of nurturing. Turning me all pale and gangly through having to fend for myself before I'm ready . . .

I've definitely gotta find some way to fight it.

Show them the error of their ways before it's too late. Before I'm blighted beyond redemption.

Woe is me, for I am undone!

Reprieve!

Ms. Jackson's out sick!

Plus I just happen to spot a spare form on her desk, buried underneath a copy of *Pride and Prejudice* and a pile of photocopied notes on William Wordsworth. I move in fast and swipe it before our substitute teacher arrives.

Phew! All's well that ends well. (Shakespeare.)

What I said re parents still stands, though.

Non-starter

Morning break. I'm emerging outta history, deep in thought.

History's so awash with bish bash bosh, you wanna lie down and die. The way our teacher tells it, it's jam-packed with self-starters. She's been banging on again about all these deprived kids, circa our age. How they educated themselves at night, by the light of a flickering candle, in a freezing cold attic, on top of a fourteen-hour working day, spent slaving as an apprentice, existing on a hunk of bread 'n cheese and tankard of ale. Yet turned themselves into inventors of world-shattering inventions, single-handed.

"No help from teachers, parents, National Curriculum, Family Income Support!" she thumps out, rising to a crescendo. "Nothing but their own, awe-inspiring, self-motivation . . ."

Dramatic pause. She stares at us over her glasses. Letting it sink in.

"You lot are like empty firework cases by

comparison," she moans. "All fancy packaging and public-health warnings. No gunpowder in your bellies!"

Could *she* be the source of my parents' misguided inspiration? Would they like me to ditch parental support altogether and put myself on the bread and cheese diet? Is that what they've got in mind? Might find it's too late. As a victim of mollycoddling at an early age, could be my success-drive mechanism's got prematurely blunted—permanently.

These deep thoughts are hogging my brain when Natalie, alias Miss News of the World (and not for her pinup potential), sidles up.

"Been invited to Ruth Bateman's party?" she lobs.

I'm caught right off guard. I wince.

I bite back the fatal, giveaway words, "Which party?" and search my brain for a flip, throwaway riposte. None comes.

"Er . . . not yet," I mutter, tight-lipped.

Natalie sighs. "Pity. You can take a friend. Was going to offer to let you take me." She shrugs and runs her eyes over me, like I'm a reject piece of pottery and she's examining me for hairline cracks. "I'll just have to find somebody who has been invited then, won't I?"

She pulls a face and slithers off in search of more worthy prey.

Urrgh . . . My throat goes into a choking spasm.

I make a sign of the cross.

As if I'd take *her*.

Ric's in the sticky bun queue. I give him a dig.

"Know Ruth Bateman's having a party?" I say, casual-sounding.

Ric's stupid mug breaks into a grin. "Yup. Halloween party. Out at her ancient, timber-framed farmhouse, that's reputed to be haunted. And Ruth's been dabbling in white witchcraft. Should be good, eh? Invites are like gold dust. Everybody'd kill for one."

Strewth—even Ric knows?

"Er—know who is going?"

"Let's see . . . Lyndsey, Ursula, Gary, Josh, Will . . . er . . . that lot. You know—the 'in' crowd."

"*In* crowd?" My stomach plummets in free fall. In that case, why've I not been invited? Instead of getting myself on the fast track for future celebrity status, have I got shunted by my peer group into a future nonentity siding? Despite all my recent efforts?

Crisis!

"So why've I not been invited?" I tremble out loud.

Ric shrugs, nonchalantly. "Dunno. I have."

Shock waves reverberate through my entire system. My mouth drops open. "What-t? *You've* got an invite? YOU?"

"Yeah." Ric looks smug. "Didn' I say?"

He puts his hand in his inside pocket, like he's performing a conjuring trick. He draws out this piece of flashy purple card with gimpy edges. He waves it under my nose. "Ta-da!"

The card's decorated with glitter pentagrams and spirals, and it's got silver spidery handwriting that's back to front. Must've taken hours to do.

"Mirror writing," he points out proudly.

I stare at that purple card and am swamped by a wave of sick, covetous loathing. All my efforts to get myself noticed! Even risking life and limb on the rugby pitch, just to prove I've got bish bash bosh. And Ric, who can hardly be bothered to breathe some days, gets an invite to this hyped-up, wanna-go-to party. Whereas I don't.

Is there no justice in the world?

"Why?" I grind.

"Makes it more mysterious."

"Not the writing, you berk!" I thunder. "YOU! Why did you get an invite and not me?"

"Put it like this," he says in this singsong voice, "some of us have got 'it' and some of us ain't. Looks like I'm an 'it' guy, mate."

"I'm off," I seethe. "Before you end up being a 'hit' guy!"

"Ha, ha! Very funny." He restrains me. "On the other hand, it could be 'cos you're just known among the girl population these days as 'Sandi's ex.' Whereas they never met Carro, did they? So me, I'm still virgin territory."

I burst out laughing. You'd have to, wouldn't you?

Only it's bitter laughter. That sort always gives me a stitch.

Ric Rites It

Why's Ruth's party so hyped up and wanna-go-to, anyway?

Truth is, parties of any sort, for our age group, in our neck of the woods, are virtually obsolete.

Just mention the words "teenage party" and parents are reaching for their palpitation pills. Not in their lounges with their new fitted carpets and leather upholstery and repro mahogany coffee tables that show every mark. Let a gang of teenagers loose? No way!

So parties are always happening somewhere else—across town, up north, down under, in girlie mags and TV soaps . . . in my dreams.

And now, here's Ruth Bateman actually throwing one. And on Halloween, with all the opportunities for devilry and shenanigans that date conjures up. And I'm not invited.

Not even short-listed. Not seeded. A weakest link.

Sandi Weston's not been invited either, though. That's some consolation.

In fact, I discover only four of the males invited go to our school—Gary, Josh, Will, and Ric.

Hmm . . . Could just about handle Gary, Josh, and Will being invited and not me. They all live out in the country and sometimes travel on the same bus as

Ruth. And are supersporting, like Ruth. (Ruth wields her hockey stick at all-state county level.)

But Ric? Where the heck does *Ric* fit in?

A few discreet phone calls. Some carefully worded text messages. Ric's little secret is revealed.

He's no more an "it" guy than I am. Ha!

No wonder he looked proud of that mirror writing. *He* did it! Yeah!

Picture it.

Seems he was boasting to Ruth in art one day last week about his skills in back-to-front calligraphy. Being a bright girl, Ruth saw an opportunity. She struck a bargain with him. He'd write *all* her invitations in return for getting *one* for himself.

Honestly, the lengths some kids'll go to to get in with the "in" crowd.

What a mug!

What's more—listen to this—he misspelled Halloween!

When they held up their invites to a mirror, everybody discovered they'd been invited to a Helloween Party!

Ho, ho! Am I splitting my sides about that. And I ain't the only one.

Not that it makes up for my lack of an invite, though.

Sigh.

I'd have given *anything* to have gone to Ruth's A-list party, and Sandi Weston not. . . .

Fancy Dress Folly

The following evening.

Brrring-brrring, brrring-brrring . . .

"Hi. 'S Ric."

"Oh? Fancy you finding the time to ring boring old me," I say, heavy on the sarcasm. "I hear your social schedule's so full, you're swatting off friends like flies. Er, *Hello* magazine rung you up, yet?"

"Very funny. Ha, ha! Listen, if you don't put a sock in it, I'm not gonna invite you."

Silence.

"What?" I swallow back an excitement rush.

"Would you repeat that?"

"You heard."

"I thought you said you're inviting me."

"Not if you're gonna keep playing the smart alec."

He is inviting me!

I turn suspicious.

"Why're you not inviting a girl-person? Thought it was your big chance. Ruth's party's been so hyped up, you'd easy find a girl to go with you. No problem. There's Natalie for a start. Trouble with Natalie though—it might be Halloween, but when you pull off the scary mask, you like to know there's somebody normal underneath."

"Find a girl?" screeches Ric. "They're laying siege to me, man! (Slight exaggeration?) That's the trouble—I'm spoiled for choice. Don't wanna make any hasty decisions I might regret later. Bound to be loads to spare at the party. I'd rather freelance. See what catches my eye when I'm there. See what little bundle Fate throws in my lap."

Personally I think Ric's got it wrong. All the best talent will arrive already spoken for. Like my mum says, all the best turkeys are pre-ordered at Christmas. But if his shaky reasoning means an invite for me . . .

"Wise decision," I say.

"You can come, then."

"Right. Okay, then. [Laid-back tone.] Fine."

Eat yer heart out, Sandi Weston! Eat yer heart out Natalie Redfern!

I *am* going!

Yeees!

"Only don't do nothing to cramp my style, or lower the tone," Ric rabbits on. "And it's fancy dress. So you'll be needing an outfit. Poundland has got some good masks, only a quid. We could go tomorrow, after school, and choose you one."

"What're you going as?"

"I was thinking of being an Egyptian mummy. We could wrap me up in bandages and—"

"A *what*? A *mummy*? Brilliant party you'd have! Propped up in a corner. Can't move. Can't eat. Can't—Hmm . . . not a *bad* idea, come to think of it."

"So what do *you* fancy going as, Clever Clogs?"

"Think I'll go as a wizard," I say.

"Hey—*I* was just thinking of saying a wizard!" he cuts in. "My mum's got this purple velvet curtain that'd make a wicked cloak. And I know where I can get one of them steeple hats, with the moon and stars already stuck on. And *I'm* the one with the invite!"

Think I'll keep any further thoughts to myself. Ric's got this nasty habit of infiltrating my original ideas and eating them hollow from the inside, like a grub.

Dressed to Kill

Well, here it is, folks! The night of All Hallows' Eve, or Samhain, to give it its witches' name. Or Helloween in Ric-speak.

I'm inspecting my party outfit in the bedroom mirror. Looks good! Even if I do say so myself. Brilliant. Dead macho, even with the sling. So cunningly original, there'll only be one of me and the rest are gonna be green with envy.

Funnily enough, getting hold of the meat cleaver

was no great hassle. I got this really authentic-looking plastic one, dirt cheap, from a joke shop. The dark blue boilersuit gave me the most problems. I finally wound up in one of those places that sells heavy machinery, like floor sanders, arc welders, and cement mixers. Boilersuits come in one size only. Large male. No trying-on facilities. Plus sales tax. Cost me a bundle. And I've had to put a belt around it. Still, worth it to look authentic. Worth it to establish my reputation as Party Animal First Class.

I practice a few gruesome expressions and strike a few terrifying poses. Excellent! I look really weirdo-scary. Especially with the talcum powder on my cheeks and Mum's eyeliner around my eyes.

I decide to try out my role on Mum, who's cooking something frozen—all unsuspecting—in the kitchen.

I creep stealthily down the stairs . . .

I crash open the kitchen door. So hard it smacks against the side wall.

I stand there on the threshold. Manic expression on my face, murder written in every line . . .

Mum looks up from the cooker. Gasps.

I await the dropped spatula, the overturned saucepan, the bloodcurdling scream.

But instead my mum's face breaks into a grin. "Oh, very good!" she claps. "What are you? Let me guess . . . Are you a Kwik-Fit fitter? Shall I sing the jingle? D'you know the dance?"

"I'm a flipping SERIAL KILLER!" I yell, wielding my plastic meat cleaver with only-just-under-control homicidal intent.

"Oooops!" Mum goes. And drops the spatula, laughing.

Pathetic!

"Er, have a nice time. But don't do anything I wouldn't do," she says.

"Like what?"

"Well, you *know*."

Innocent expression. "No," I say, winding her up.

"Don't get up to any hanky-panky your dad and I wouldn't approve of."

I do a puzzled frown. "You mean like killing people and butchering them?"

Groan.

"Right-o. Got the picture. Teenage depravity's okay, butchering people's not. Got that."

I mutter this over to myself, like a mantra:

"Teenage depravity okay; butchering people not."

"When are you going to grow up?" Mum groans.

"Er, thought you just warned me off 'hanky-panky'—that is, losing my childish innocence? Can't have it both ways—"

I duck hastily as Mum threatens to brain me with the frying pan.

Ooooh . . . can't wait to bish my bosh!

Towing the Party Line

"Don't yer just love Halloween-type tack?" Ric's blathering on. "Them glow-in-the-dark cardboard skeletons, plastic cobwebs, witches' hats, pumpkin heads. Woo-oo! Gets my adrenaline going! Lights the 'wick' in wicked!"

I sigh. Wish he'd put a sock in it! He's getting on my "wick." Funny, I've been looking forward to this party for days. Wound myself up into a state of excitement and expectation not revisited since Christmas circa age six. And now I have to start getting bad vibes. When it's too late to back out. When we're in Ric's mum's car and nearly there.

"Know when you're stuck at home on Halloween?" Ric's driveling on. "Always think you're missing out, don't yer? You picture a forest clearing with hooded figures doing devil dancing and incanting spells. Or you're wishing somebody'd dared you to go into a churchyard. And the bells are tolling midnight. And it's all rotting headstones and decomposing flesh. And flitting bats and white ghost lights hovering over open graves. Woo-oo!"

"Yeah," I mutter. "When I was a kid."

"And now here's you an' me, gonna grab a slice of the action ourselves. Halloweening it in Ruth's ancient, half-timbered farmhouse. There it is! Cor, look at that! Spook-y, eh? Spooook-yyy!"

Ric's fully revved up. Ready to go, partying with the paranormal. Me, I'm so tensed up you could stick me in a display at Madame Tussaud's and nobody'd spot the difference.

I let Ric lead the way. Off he goes, eagerly shuffling down the hallway to the party venue—Ruth's kitchen. But when he gets to the door, he pulls up short. His mouth drops open. He's got an expression on his face like some old tramp who's gasping for some coffee, only to find his favourite greasy spoon's been turned into a beauty parlor.

"Flip me!" he mutters. "Have we died and gone to church?"

I peer over his shoulder. See what he means. This party's a Halloween tack–free zone. Ruth's decked the kitchen out with whacking great bunches of greenery hanging off the beams. And flower displays and dozens of flickering tea lights and candles, grouped artistically. Quite nice, actually. Surprising, though.

I sniff. There's this strong whiff of lavender. It's like we've accidentally got locked inside my grandma's airing cupboard.

The penny drops. "Did you say Ruth's into white witchcraft?"

"So?"

"Well, I think you'll find white witches are into

115

goodness, calm, and clean, healthy living. That sorta stuff. We sorta overlooked that fact."

Ric scowls. "Could be just a clever front."

It's not.

There are two Harry Potters, so far, one wizard, a felon with a noose around his neck, and three Buffy the Vampire Slayers (only minus the drop-dead-gorgeous factor). They're standing around, looking out of place. Eyeing us, the new arrivals, in sulky-faced silence.

Ruth's got this white witch outfit on. It's a short, sleeveless burlap tunic. Like an ancient Briton. She's got sandals on her feet with her tree-trunk legs left bare. And there's a wreath of artificial flowers rammed on her head.

She swoops on us. Hauls us in. Runs her eyes over us.

"What're you, exactly? Are you a Kwik-Fit fitter?"

I cringe. Not again! Why's everybody being so *stupid*? Would a Kwik-Fit fitter have talcum powder on his cheeks and eyeliner around his eyes? Well, would he?

"No," I grind. I hold up my meat cleaver. "I'm a serial killer, actually."

"Oh, yah, right! One serial killer," Ruth brays. "And one—"

"Bog roll!" shouts one of the Potters.

There's a ripple of sniggers.

"Mummy, you berk!" Ric glowers threateningly.

"Of course you are," says Ruth.

I'm shuffling with embarrassment. Two blokes arriving together, and one of 'em's wrapped in bog roll. Ric decided to be an Egyptian mummy after all. (I suspect his mum vetoed the velvet curtain. Plus, he got hold of an Egyptian mummy mask, which solved the eating and talking problem.) Only then he had this "brilliant" idea about paper being cheaper than bandages. And he's given me the responsibility for holding him together. A giant reel of Sellotape's weighing down one of the sixteen pockets of my boilersuit. Bog roll being, as any mortal with half a brain would know, designed to be torn off. . . .

D'you wonder he's been giving me bad vibes? D'you wonder they're increasing by the second?

The doorbell rings again. Ric and I shuffle farther into the room. Ruth returns with Gary Grant and Lyndsey.

"Cor!" goes Ric. "*Phwoar!*"

Lyndsey's got a silver frock on. It's short. It's got these narrow straps and—ooooh! Ric's right—*phwoar*!

"Don't know what she's supposed to be," Ric drools in my ear, "but she's got *my* vote!"

Gary's outfit strikes a chill. He's dressed in black trousers and a white, frilly-fronted shirt and black bow tie that must be his dad's. Around his neck he's slung a vampire mask. Must've got it from Poundland. But teamed with that outfit it looks dead racy. Dead cool. All for a quid!

My mouth goes dry with envy. Why didn't I think of that?

"Another Buffy and . . . a vampire she's out to slay!" Ruth announces.

Some dweeb claps (think it's one of those Potters again). Others join in. Lyndsey and Gary take a bow. Like a couple of superstars arriving at the Oscars.

I drop my tacky plastic meat cleaver behind a log basket. I chew my lip. The party animal inside me's just got up and slunk away. Found a quiet corner to lie down and die.

A couple more wizards turn up. More white witches, dressed like Ruth, a pagan raver in flashing devil's horns, two more Harry Potters. Three Hermiones.

Ruth's parents come fussing in. They station themselves one at each end of the kitchen. Then go through emergency fire drill procedures, like a couple of airline flight attendants.

"In case of candles setting fire to greenery or curtains . . . or one of you," they go, "fire extinguisher is by the stove [they point]. A bucket of water is by the dresser [point]. Please abandon the party in an orderly fashion by the nearest exit. Either by the back door [point] or window [point]. Assemble on the back lawn, where a roll call will be taken. Thank you for your attention. Okay, go ahead and have a good time, kids! But remember, we'll be in the front sitting room, should you need us. Just give us a call."

Embarrassing silence.

Well, how's anybody supposed to get a party going when their elbows have been nailed to their sides by "calm," "goodness," and parental approval?

If in doubt, stuff your mouth. Seems to be the general theory.

Shock number two. Not a bacon frazzle, cheesy puff, BBQ beef, or scrap of anything even remotely crisplike. No fun-size bangers. No tricky toasty treats. Not even a can of Coke! All E numbers and caffeine have been given the old shazzam. There's zilch to nosh, 'cept baskets of assorted nuts, bowls of seeds, and organic fruit looking, er, *organic*. And to stop us choking on all that bird food, it's either apple juice, homemade lemonade, or elder flower cordial. Take yer pick.

No comfort eating, no caffeine boost for us tonight.

"If this is how the A-list parties, count me out," I groan.

"Aw, just give it time," says Ric.

"For what? Ruth's got *sparklers* for later, has she?"

"Yum, yum," brays one of the Hermiones above the sound of chomping nuts and grinding seeds. "These are very good nuts, Ruth, aren't they? Look at the size of these Brazils. Did you get them wholesale?"

"Holland and Barrett, actually," says Ruth.

A show-off wizard starts testing them between his finger and thumb, like a nut connoisseur. Ric flicks a hazelnut like a clown.

Was he *deliberately* aiming at Lyndsey's cleavage? He's apologizing. Claiming not. Oh yeah?

"Er, lovely candles." That's me, being smarmy. Demonstrating *I've* got some social skills. Even if I did only get my boot in the door as a friend of an invitee.

"Oh, just cheap tea lights from Ikea." Ruth smirks modestly. But she's looking pleased with me. She cocks her head, like she's expecting more.

"Must be how you've arranged them, then. Er, reflecting in the mirrors, that's so, er, good."

Nods of agreement all around.

"Yah." Ruth looks even more pleased with me. Her head stays cocked.

Hey, I've done *my* bit! Try Gary Grant. He's not made a single whole-group contribution so far. He's letting himself be distracted by Lyndsey trying to shake the hazelnut out of her bra.

I mix myself a cocktail. Elder flower cordial base. Daring dash of lemonade and adventurous shot of apple. Yuck!

My restless feeling's worse than ever. Is this *all* we're gonna do? All evening? Stand around doing conversation, like we're practicing for GCSE orals?

I grab another fistful of nuts. They're going down so fast, you'd think there'd been a ban on imports.

To be honest, if this is what a mature A-list party's like, it's dead disappointing. I was expecting a bit more edge. Chance to move up a gear. Expand my personality. Cut a dash. Not just stand around feeling like an awkward kid in a boilersuit that's half a dozen sizes too big.

Ric's just taken a surreptitious swipe at a cheeky Harry Potter who's ripped a piece off his funeral wrappings to clean his glasses.

"This party's dying on its feet," Ric hisses as I'm doing running repairs with the Sellotape.

I roll up my eyeballs, miming, "It's already expired."

"What we need's a *happening*," he says. "A-S-A-P. Got any ideas?"

"Too late. It's already R-I-P."

"Wha'?"

"Rest in Peace. Dead and Buried."

Groan. "Got a pack of cards? Could do 'em some of yer David Blaine–type card tricks."

"Take more than card tricks to liven this lot up."

"Well *you're* supposed to be clever; you think of something."

"A defibrilator?"

"Wha'?"

"Machine for shocking your heart into pumping again once it's stopped."

Bigger groan. "You're useless, you are. All sarcasm. No action. Ask around, see if anybody's brought a firecracker."

"And what d'you reckon we'd do with that? Drop it inside Ruth's knickers?"

Ric's eyes light up, rotate, and go *ping*.

"Jackpot!" he grins.

Knew I shouldn't have come.

Two Cackling Hens and an Apple Tree

A piercing shriek! Sounds like some girl-person's being molested. My heart skips a beat.

Oh no, Ric's not . . . has he?

I catch his eye. "That *you*?" I mouth, sternly.

"That *you*?" he's mouthing back, excited.

But the shrieking's nothing to do with either of us. A white witch called Sophie's pointing at the kitchen window and going heavy on the dramatics.

It's not a flasher—false alarm. Only a couple of old-fashioned-type witches in long black cloaks, steeple hats, and hag masks with warts. They're cackling and giggling and going, "Woooo-oo."

I grin. "A normal happening, at last. About time."

Ruth's got this haughty expression on her face though. "It's a couple of trick-or-treating, black-witch gate-crashers!" She starts waving her arms around, like she's shooing a stray dog off the hockey pitch. And booming, "Go a-way! You're trespassing! Go a-way!"

Her popularity's at stake, though. 'Cause everybody else wants them in. "Let 'em in, Ruth! Go on, don't be a spoilsport, let 'em in!"

Ruth's huffing and tutting. Going all red in the face. But she'll have to let 'em in, or somebody else will. She opens the door.

In they leap. Cackling. Screeching. Shattering the karma to smitheereens. Whipping out bribes from under their cloaks. Wow, a bumper pack of Walkers Assorted Shortbread! A tin of Pringles Potato Chips! A six-pack of Coke!

They get *mobbed*.

Not by Ric and me, though. I grab Ric's arm. I yank him back. "Don't encourage 'em!"

I've twigged who they are. I'm getting an allergic reaction. A compulsion to make a sign of the cross. If that's not Sandi Weston and Natalie Redfern, I'll eat my plastic meat cleaver!

"I'm livid with the pair of 'em. This is supposed to be an *exclusive* do," I snarl. "Ruth didn't invite *them*. They don't even qualify as friends of invitees. Look at 'em—scattering E numbers and caffeine. Taking over the show. Flipping nerve!"

"Yeah," Ric grouches. "And I had to wear my fingers to the bone, writing all them invites, to get our invite!"

Ruth's got this disgusted expression on her face. Like a cook who's watching all her lovely pies being snatched from under her nose and used as missiles.

"Hey, Ruth's got this big old apple tree in her garden!" (Natalie's dulcet tones.) "Why don't we all go out and *hug* it?"

Why hug a tree? Search me. I'm trying to start up a discussion on the point. But there's this mass stampede into the dark, muddy garden, where it stinks of rotting vegetation and cat piss. Ric and I get swept along on the tidal wave.

A bossy wizard forms everybody into a big circle. Next thing you know they're all dancing and capering around that apple tree, like you'd think civilization was never invented.

Then the hugging starts. First the apple tree. Then any old tree. Then each other. Roaring wizards start chasing shrieking witches around the bushes. And vice versa. A lethal cocktail of brimstone and hormone crackles in the air.

I'm not joining in, though. No way. I'm just standing

here. Nursing my sling and demonstrating that I'm above all this. Sandi Weston and Natalie Redfern caused this mayhem. I'm not letting *my* actions be manipulated by the likes of *them*.

"Oooops, 'scuse me!" This Hermione suddenly barges into me. Accidentally on purpose, I presume. She grabs me around the middle. Pretending to steady herself. Swamps me in a cloud of flowery scent. "What's up, sulky chops? Can't yer run with that sling on?" she challenges in my ear.

On second thought, no point in missing out on *all* the action, is there?

"Try me!" I growl, and I kick start.

Phew, that's loosened me up! That's got the adrenaline going! I'm starting to enjoy myself at last. This is more like it!

Next I'm going after a black-cloaked, Sandi-shaped hell-hag. Intention: spot of serve-her-right terrorizing. Wish I'd hung on to my meat cleaver!

"I know it's you, Sandi Weston!" I gasp. "Found your niche, haven't you? Creating havoc!"

I grab her hag mask, ready to go, "Arrrgh! Yuck!"

at the sight of her real face.

Guess what! I'm staring into the face of . . . Natalie.

"YOU! Urrrgh!"

I spin on my heel. I peer into the darkness. "Where's Sandi?"

"I'm not with Sandi—it's Louisa and me."

"What?"

"Sandi's gone to the school concert."

"Wha-*t*?"

"She's at the concert, cloth-ears. That bloke Andy was going. One she fancies. Him from Year Twelve. One she packed *you* in for. Sandi says she's outgrown Halloween parties, anyway."

I stagger away into the darkness, clutching my stomach. My gut feels like Natalie's just fed it through a sausage machine and twisted it into chipolatas.

"Oi! Psssst!"

It's Ric, hissing at me from the kitchen door. He's inside, pulling faces and beckoning frantically. "I've been in the loo and pinched the bog roll," he gasps. "Come inside quick and patch me up!"

"Told ya you should've brought your jeans, you stupid prat!"

He tosses the roll at me. "Shut up and get patching."

It takes the whole roll.

And just think, at this minute, Sandi Weston's dressed up to the nines. Soaking up culture. At a concert. With her new boyfriend—Andy. Bet he's reeking of cologne and inviting her to share his program. *I* could have been improving *my* brain. Brushing up on *my* musical appreciation at the school concert. That's what's *mature*. That's where the bish bash bosh is. Instead I'm at this tacky party, getting all hot and sweaty, capering around trees in a man-size boilersuit. And playing undertaker to an unravelling mummy.

Spooked

I'm leaning on the stove, quietly scorching and festering.

We're all back indoors now. Depositing mud.

The party's in full swing. That bucket of water for emergency firefighting's been commandeered for apple bobbing. It's sloshed all over the floor.

Somebody's set up a makeshift séance on the dining room table, with an upturned tumbler and the alphabet written on paper napkins. And some other berk's just run around trying to blow out all the candles. Thinks that might encourage Ruth's (alleged) household ghost to appear, as if any ghost in its right mind would show up in a scene like this. There's so much smoke it's set off the smoke alarm. Causing Ruth's parents to come charging in, armed with a whistle and shouting "Nobody panic! Nobody panic!" Trying to order us back outside.

That finally sorted, a CD player's materialized. It's thumping out background music for a who-can-do-the-most-grotesque-dancing contest. They all look like winners.

Me, I'm right out of sync. Can't help it. Blame Natalie's revelations. Otherwise I'd have been in the thick of this. Loving it. Can't now. (Sigh.) Would I really rather be at a concert instead, though? Nah, that neither, to be honest. (Sigh.) Don't know where I want to be right now. (Even deeper sigh.) Has innocent happiness floated out of my life for good? Got replaced forever more by this feeling of angst, pinching and nipping at my brain like a pair of badly fitting shoes?

"Oi! You! Party pooper! Shift yer backside off that stove. We need you for this game."

I heave myself off the stove. (Sigh that sounds like it's been dredged up from the icy waters of the North Atlantic.)

Turns out it's only a mind reading game. The one where you have to draw a symbol on a piece of paper. Like a moon or a star or a cross. The others try and guess which one you've drawn.

Could be worse. Well, so I think.

How wrong can you get?

"Cheat! She's cheating! Cheating!!" I fling. How else could *Natalie* have right guessed what I've drawn that many times?

"I can read your mind!" she shrieks, eyes drilling into my skull.

Urrgh! I'm quitting this game.

Let them groan!

My mental defenses are in urgent need of repair and reinforcement. Breached by the likes of Natalie!

"It means we're mentally compatible!" she lobs after me. "Got that? Mentally compatible!"

Eeeek. There's this note in her voice. Sounds like it could crumble castle walls! Burst the locks off prison doors! Infiltrate an iron-lined safe box in the vaults of the Bank of England! I exaggerate not!

Panic stations!

Where to hide from her?

Five minutes later. I'm crouched in fetal position behind the big log basket, in a highly nervous state. I've given Natalie the slip for now. But somebody's just been in the loo and discovered the total lack of bum-wipe. And figured out where it's gone. And now, guess what? Ric-the-human-bog-roll's being stripped, piece by piece. Causing great hilarity and amusement to everybody, bar himself.

I watch him fighting a pathetic rear-guard action toward the hall.

Enough's enough! And I've had more than enough.

I dart across Natalie-infested waters and follow Ric.

•　　•　　•

"You might at leasta worn *Calvins*!"

I thrust my mobile under his nose. "Quick. Ring your mum. Tell her to get the car around. Pronto. Emergency alert. We've gotta get outta here. *I'm* an endangered species, and you—*you're* no longer even decent!"

"Keep your hair on," he hisses. "I'm waiting for Ruth."

Ruth appears, right on cue, smiling a smile like a nursery nurse. She strides to the dog gate barring the stairs. Officiously tosses aside her parents' KEEP OUT sign and unbolts it.

"Come along, Ric," she coos. She holds out an encouraging hand, while modestly looking the other way.

A tattered and torn figure, like a corpse that's been accidentally dropped off a stretcher and fought over by stray dogs, emerges from behind a display of pampas grass.

"Er, *after* you, Ruth," it says.

Barred from following, it's my turn to nip behind the pampas grass.

Five minutes later they come down again.

What *does* Ric look like?

He's wearing droopy cords and the sorta sweater you wouldn't want to wear at home alone, in case you accidentally caught sight of yourself in a mirror.

"Ruth's brother's," he mutters, looking sheepish.

"Dan's away at university." Ruth runs a satisfied eye over Ric. "Just a couple of items he left behind. No problem. Only, make sure you look after that sweater, Ric. My gran knitted it."

"We'd better be going now," I say firmly. "Ring your mum, Ric."

"What? *Leave?*" Ruth gives this winded gasp. Then she snorts in air and starts booming it back at me in such a fashion that a megaphone would be redundant. "And break up my party? When it's going really well? When Will and Kirsty say it's the best party they've ever been to? Why do you have to be such a SPOILSPORT? Why can't you be more like Ric? At least *he* makes an effort. You just turn up dressed as a Kwik-Fit fitter and go sulk, sulk, sulk. I don't know why he brought you. No wonder you're Sandi Weston's *ex!*"

Silence. Then tittering and sniggering starts up from six heads poking around the kitchen door.

I'm reeling from the blast. My ego feels like it's been shot to pieces.

The sheer *unfairness* of this Ruth-person's left me speechless. All the dosh I wasted on my outfit! The time, effort, and ingenuity I put into it! The totally unappreciated *originality*! The grand aims I started out with. Cutting the mustard. Bishing the bosh. Turning myself into Party Animal First Class!

Remind me in the future to tell Ruth Bateman where to *stick* her candles.

"Hey, he's not *that* bad," Ric mutters back at Ruth.

No consolation there. Useless object's just defending his own taste in friends. Not me.

I glower at him. I can't get home without a lift from his mum. He knows it. And now I'm even more *determined* we're going.

Ruth glowers at me. Just as determined we're not.

Ric's shifty little eyes flicker between the two of us.

This is a test of your loyalty, mate.

It's precisely one hour and thirty-seven minutes before we're finally in the car. Half of that time I spent on a shelf behind a wax jacket in Ruth's broom cupboard under the stairs. Hiding from Natalie. The other half I'm not even prepared to go into. The friendship of a lifetime (reputed to have started in the womb, when Ric's mum met mine at prenatal classes) is hanging by a thread. My mouth's zipped up as tight as my overall pockets. My body language alone could get me arrested on suspicion of homicide.

"Oh, look!" Ric's mum's glancing in her driving mirror as we bump away down the potholed drive. "There's a witch on the doorstep, waving. Is she just waving you boys good-bye? Or do you think she wants me to stop?"

I turn. I squint through the back window. Sweat breaks out on my forehead. It's *Natalie*. "Step on the gas, Mrs. Cooper!"

Ric's ugly mug leers at me over the passenger seat. "Think you've made a hit there. Reckon Natalie's after you."

"Ooooh-er!" goes his mum.

"She's *not*!" I yell in hot denial. "She hates me!

Everybody knows she hates me! Everybody knows she's got her sights set on Diabolical Haircut in Year Twelve."

Ric shrugs. "Sometimes you've gotta lower your sights. Looks like Natalie's gone and lowered hers, mate."

I make a sign of the cross. I swat the air around me. I'm trying to beat off the ghastly truth.

Natalie! Urrrgh! She used to hate me. What's gone wrong? I was comfortable with that. It was like an acknowledgment that I was a different species.

What's happening to everybody suddenly? Seems like there's not a single soul you can trust to act in character. Not your parents. Not your friends. Not your enemies. Not even your flipping self!

And where has my appearance at Ruth's party left me in the It Guy stakes?

Eliminated, I presume.

Is there any point in trying?

Six

Video Nasties

Sock Warfare

SATURDAY MORNING. The morning after the party. I'm feeling fragile. Inside out. Back to front. Handle with care. My feet are bare. Urrrgh. Talk about rough terrain. You'd never let a pair as ugly as mine run around bare by choice. Not unless you were a masochist.

"Where's all my casual socks?" I groan.

"Drawer?" says Mum, with nil conviction.

"One pair of Power Rangers," I grind. "Children's shoe size eleven to thirteen."

"Dryer?"

"The dryer is empty."

"Under your bed?"

"I'm talking *clean* socks."

"Washing machine, then," she says calmly. "You

141

put them through that hole in the front. Add detergent, click a few switches—hey, presto—clean socks."

"I'm not joking!" I snarl. Can't she see I'm in need of maternal comfort and support?

"Neither am I."

"Wash my own socks?"

"Then you'd always know where you stood, sockwise. Not be basing your supply on the vagaries of other people." She eyeballs me shamelessly. "He who controls his own socks takes an important step toward controlling his own life."

I bury my face in my hands.

"Supposing we negotiate?" she says.

I groan.

This is serious stuff she's trotting out. Must've been reading it somewhere. Parenting magazine? Women's magazine? Sunday supplement? Suspect such magazines are riddled with hints and tips on how to promote maturity in your teenage boy. "Six easy skills for living, and how *your* kid can acquire them"—that sorta thing.

This is not what I need right now.

Sounds like she's actually got a *plan*. Forcing me to become master of my own destiny through control of my homework, my cereal supply, and now, my socks! Well, no way. I'm not gonna be manipulated. I'm fighting back. Not even gonna think about washing my own socks till . . . Stop! I'm not even gonna fall into the trap of thinking when I'll start thinking about it. Sock washing is one adult skill I'm in no rush to acquire.

I'd rather declare Sock Warfare. We'd soon see who surrendered first to the putrid smell of my neglected feet. I'd release them from my shoes on all occasions likely to gain maximum effect. Like during her favorite soap.

On the other hand . . . I part my fingers and eye the washing machine's gaping mouth. I sigh. Maybe I'd better have a go at getting the hang of it, just in case? As emergency backup. My mum's never been a pushover.

"You're obviously upset this morning," she says. "Got a problem you'd like to discuss?"

Help! I exit the kitchen, double fast.

Spell Check

Brrring-brrring, brrring-brrring . . .

"He-llo."

"You've got something of mine," hisses this girlie voice.

It's Natalie! My hand shakes so much I nearly drop the phone. Now what?

"I don't think so!" I gasp.

"Oh, yes you have. Go on, ask me what."

"What?"

"A hair off my head. I slipped it into your pocket last night. At the party."

"Why? Why'd you go and do that?"

"To bind us together," she says in this weirdoid voice. "As long as you've got my hair, you can't escape me. It's a spell."

I groan. "Halloween's over, Natalie."

"Our minds are compatible, remember?" she says.

"Cut the crap. Which pocket?"

"Ah, that would be telling."

"There's sixteen pockets in that boilersuit!" I seethe. "Which flipping one?"

"*Sixteen* pockets? Exactly. And just one little hair. You'll never find it. Never! You are mine to command! You'll never escape me! Never! Ha, ha! Ha, ha! He's got *sixteen* pockets!!"

She collapses into hysterical laughter. Another girl's voice joins in.

I'd recognize that shrieking laughter anywhere— Sandi Weston!

"Go swallow a bulb of garlic—both of you!" I yell.

I cut them off.

That's all I need.

Trouble with girls is, you never know when you should take them seriously. Sometimes they don't even know when they're being serious themselves, that's my theory. When they're laughing their heads off, though, that's when you know you oughta watch out.

So I find the boilersuit. It's where I abandoned it last night—in a crumpled heap on my bedroom floor.

I rummage quickly through all the pockets. Nothing but an empty reel of Sellotape.

Natalie's right. To find a single hair, you'd have to turn every single pocket inside out and go over them one by one with a magnifying glass.

I picture me doing that.

I imagine the girls' raucous shrieks as *they* picture me doing that.

No way!

I sit back on my haunches. I scowl at the ransacked boilersuit. This calls for a cool, calm deployment of the old gray cells. . . . Hmm . . . Knowing girls, it's more than likely there's no hair there at all and they're just having me on.

On the other hand, supposing there is a hair? Well, so what? This witchcraft stuff's just a loada mumbo jumbo.

What's the problem?

Prickling hairs on the back of my neck. That's what. Fingers twitching into a sign of the cross.

Better be on the safe side. . . . We're talking Natalie here.

Set fire to the thing?

Not at that price. Not when I paid for it myself.

Inspiration strikes. A sly grin spreads from ear to ear.

I'll loan it to Ric.

Transfer the spell and see what happens.

Ric's got a hide like a rhino. Let him cope.

Brrring-brrring, brrring-brrring . . .

"Ric, me old mate! How're you doing this morning?"

"Can't decide," he drones, "if I should give Ruth a ring now and ask her out, or if I should wait till tomorrow, or if I should e-mail, or wait till I take her brother's stuff back. Whatya think?"

Ruth? What's the fathead blathering on about?

"Listen," I hiss, "sounds like you're suffering from a chronic attack of postparty brain disorder. Try standing on your head for half an hour. That should cure it."

"*Wha'?*"

"Take my advice, do nothing till normal service is resumed."

"Wha'?"

"Listen, howdya like to borrow my boilersuit?"

"Why? Wha' for? How'd that help me decide?"

"It wouldn't. I just want it outta the house."

Suspicious hesitation.

"Your mum not know you bought it, then?"

"No questions asked."

"No buying involved?"

"None."

A sigh. "Okay. You can bring it around."

Yeees!

Some things do go according to plan.

There's this diabolical caterwauling thumping out of Ric's kitchen. It's this female pop star who shall remain nameless, circa not much more than our age. Real teeny-bopper, cringe-cringe, fingers-down-the-throat stuff. I raise my eyebrows. I reel in horror.

Ric looks shifty. He shakes his head. "Nothing to do with me, mate."

We're just heading up the stairs to his room when the kitchen door flies open. Ric's dad takes a nosey out to see who's there.

"Oh," he says, "it's you."

"Er, yeah, Mr. Cooper. Only me."

"Guess who that is? Hey?" He flings the kitchen door wide open and wafts the sound out so we can all share.

I smile feebly.

"Cor," he goes. "She's a bit of all right, hey?" He rolls his eyes. Pouts up his lips. Makes wavy motions with his hands. "*Phwoar!* Hey? *Phwoar!* Bet you both *fancy* her, hey?"

I clear my throat. "Er—" I do my feeble smile again.

Ric grabs my arm. We both bolt up the stairs, two at a time.

There's some matters you don't rib your mates over. You wipe them from your brain, like they never happened. This one's for wiping. Definitely.

Tight-lipped, Ric selects one of his latest CDs and whacks it in.

Pumps it up loud. Dead loud.

It's tragic, really. Ric's dad used to be stern and distant. He'd fix you with this steely stare that said, "I know what you've been up to, you little hooligan."

Had you squirming, even when you'd done nothing. I respected that. That's cool.

Now it's like Shakespeare's Macbeth has gone for audience appeal by rattling off jokes and doing a tap dance.

Why do parents do it?

In for a Duck

The following morning. I'm exuding angst and depression at the kitchen table. My growing-out hair's sticking up at the back like a peacock's tail. I've tried washing it, gelling it, glueing it down with hairspray, all to no avail. What's more, it's Sunday. Inevitably going to be followed by Monday. Math homework's rubbing blisters on my conscience. And despite all my efforts of recent weeks, my social diary's bare.

Slump.

The back door bursts open. Dad jogs in with the newspaper under his arm, followed by a blast of cold, invigorating air. I shrivel inside my dressing gown.

Dad's more awash with bish bash bosh than an American athlete who's won Olympic gold. He's so charged up, he's running around the kitchen like the Energizer rabbit.

Wish he'd never dug out his tracksuit. It's enough to make you sick. Here's me—the future generation. And all my quest for bish bash bosh has resulted in so far is a sore ear, broken collarbone, hairdo that passed its "sell by" date a month and a half ago. And now—the curse of Natalie!

There's gotta be something wrong here, somewhere.

"Mrs. J wants to know if you'll take Hannibal for a run," he says.

I yawn. I grunt. I droop even farther over my cereal bowl. Raising the spoon's too big an effort.

It's not what you actually *do* that makes you tired, is it? It's grieving over what you couldn't muster up enough energy and initiative to do. That's what really knackers you.

Not that I mind too much, taking our neighbor's

rottweiler, Hannibal, for a walk. He's a good boy. At least *he* appreciates me. And he doesn't have much of a home life. He's bullied by an old poodle and a Persian cat.

So I decide I'll take Hannibal to the park.

And I'll take the camcorder with me, just in case.

There's this new camcorder club started up at school, and I'm keen to get some entertaining footage to show at next Tuesday's meeting.

Not very bish bash bosh. I know.

But you can't be upping your profile all the time. And look where that's got me so far, anyway.

Er, it's my dad's camcorder, to be precise. But only in the sense that he paid for it. Means I'll have to go through the rigmarole of asking for it, though.

"Borrow the camcorder, Dad?" etc.

Dad overreacts in typical fashion. Throws his hands up and mimes exaggerated alarm (he thinks that's funny). Then he goes, "Tut, tut, I don't know about that. Supposing you break it, eh? Think I'd better come along and give you some advice?"

Now that really is funny. I have to remind him he'd

never even have deciphered the instruction manual without my help. And I tell him I'm still not convinced he knows his white balance from his shutter speed and his focus from his zoom.

He gets so offended, I'm in danger of having blown it. So I go, "Got some math homework I'd like your expert advice on, though."

Amazing! Here I am, offering him a surefire father-son bonding opportunity. But he's out of the kitchen door faster than greased lightning. Saying he hasn't showered yet.

I don't ask much from my parents. Just my creature comforts taken care of, an adequate supply of dosh, and the occasional spot of help with math homework. Can they deliver? Nah.

Got the camcorder, though.

Not many humans in the park this morning. Too dull. Too chilly. There's just a few bored-looking dads trundling little kids. Bundled off out of the way while Sunday lunch gets cooked. I smile kindly at the kids. Used to be one of them myself, not that long ago.

'Course, the park was more fun back then. Not *all* the swings were vandalized and the slide was still operational. Provided your dad inspected it first.

I whistle to Hannibal and we head for the duck pond. Hannibal goes gallumphing ahead. That dog's got *energy*. He's already covered ten times more ground than I have. Yawn. It wears you out just watching him. Nothing wrong with *his* bish bash bosh count either.

Yawn. Yawwwn.

Wish he'd do something worth videoing. Get chased up a tree by a squirrel. Slip on a banana skin and perform an amazing series of double somersaults. Or—

Zap!

My body's gone all quivery, like a shaft of negative energy's just passed through it.

There they stand. Water's edge. Surrounded by mallards and common pochards (ducks, to you igno-ramuses). This pair is wearing jeans and chunky hug-me sweaters. It's Sandi with Andy. He of the stick-insect legs.

154

Sandi's got a Sainsbury's sliced-bread bag dangling from her hand.

They're feeding the ducks!

How *could* she?

My insides knot. I forget to breathe out.

Who introduced her to feeding the ducks? ME! Feeding the ducks was *mine*! That used to be ME standing there. But she told ME she was *bored* with it.

Sandi'd rather feed the ducks with him? A twerp who's not even breaking the bread into swallowable pieces. Who's not even duck-friendly!

She's looking up at him. Yuck! Revolting, simpering smile fuses with mega-conceited God's-gift-to-girls smirk.

Hello. You're not, mate! Not a patch on *me*. Just taller and older. Not that much taller. Not that much older. Bet you still can't get served in a pub!

What to do? Slink away before they spot me? Move forward and confront them?

Actually, no choice. My vibrating rage's riveted me to the spot.

For the rest of this scene I'm just an innocent, riveted-to-the-spot bystander. Who just happens to have a camcorder in his hand. And the initiative to start recording. Rest is pure fate. Me—innocent. Apart from supplying the rottweiler. Who I admit's illegally off the leash, packed full of hormones, and out of control.

Apart from that, I'm innocent.

Loud, throaty bark (off camera). Hannibal's just spotted Sandi. She's his pal. They share this peculiar passion for cheese 'n onion potato chips.

Sandi turns around. Registers shock-horror. Lets out one of her seriously piercing shrieks. (Sort that could pierce eardrums and shatter windows within a radius of half a mile). Appears not to have recognized Hannibal. Instead has mistaken him for the Hound of the Baskervilles.

Pan camera as half a ton of rippling doggie muscle charges across the grass with big pink tongue lolling out. Obvious intention: greeting Sandi and frisking her for potato chips.

Begin to track as Hannibal gathers loads of momentum. Close-up on powerful hind quarters braced for rearing and big front paws soaring, ready to plonk themselves on Sandi's shoulders.

Wide on Sandi backing away . . .

Dog meeting Girl. Paws connecting with shoulders.

BOOMFF!

Zoom in on Sandi toppling like a felled tree. Exiting into pond, base over apex. Smacking water bum first.

Focus on Sandi on her back in the duckweed. Arms and legs waving like she's doing the dying fly.

Pandemonium! Squawking, thrashing, splashing, barking! Hannibal frolicking like it's some great game.

Pan over to twerp. Doubled up. Literally. Laughing so much he's not making any attempt to haul Sandi out. Useless prat!

Pan back to Sandi floundering out unaided. Jeans leaking water. Strands of something green and nasty dangling off the back of her sweater.

Still clutching the Sainsbury's bread bag, though.

Spotting Andy still laughing fit to choke himself. Not anymore!

Sandi thwacking him around the head with the bag of stale bread.

Yeah, go fer it, Sand!

Wrapper bursting. All over twerp!

Dwell on no-longer-smiling mug!

Focus on Hannibal, shaking off pond water and charging in. (Oooops! See that? That dog'll stick his snout *anywhere* for a bit of soggy bread.)

Cut to Sandi wrestling with twerp. Pushing him. Shoving him. Dragging him. Attempting to get her own back and give *him* a ducking.

Andy fighting back. But having to fend off both Sandi and sodden, prancing, rearing, probing, soggy-bread-crazed teenage rottweiler.

Zoom in on Andy's brand-new-looking Adidas trainers, teetering centimeters from the pond.

Will they? Won't they?

Wow. Slight shaking of footage at this point, excitement induced.

Refocus on twerp's legs, ankle-deep in pond water.

Trainers submerged. Linger on trainers submerged. More shaking footage, laughter induced.

I'm so carried away filming twerp furiously bailing out his trainers, it's a second or two before I realize Sandi's suddenly spotted me.

Is now actually staggering across the grass toward me. As fast as her waterlogged jeans'll let her . . .

Homicidal intent!

Help!

I stand my ground and continue to film her for a second or two. Catch the bit where she's waving her fist at me—it's too juicy to miss.

Then I whistle to Hannibal and we skedaddle.

Him with the bread bag dangling out of his mouth, like a trophy. Me clutching the video camera, like I've just stolen the crown jewels.

Revenge! Revenge!

"Where's your dignity and maturity now, Twerp-face?" I yell. Does he hear me?

Wow! That's reinvigorated me! That's set my feel-good pheremones doing backward flips and shouting "Come on! Come on!" I've caught the whole flipping lot! Registered it for posterity. Mine to rerun at the flick of a switch. Slow-mo, fast-mo, rewind, pause—the entertainment potential is *endless*!

Repercussions

"You've got a visitor."

Sunday evening and I'm up in my room. Math homework's taken care of. I'm sprawling across my bed, chilling out, CD blaring.

Mum pokes her head around the door, pulling warning faces.

"It's *Sandi*. You friends again?" she mouths.

Trouble! Did I really think Sandi'd let me get away with it?

"Tell her to come up," I shout over the music. "And mind your own biz," I mouth back.

"I already have." Sandi marches straight in. Not giving me a second to get my brain into defense mode. She's wearing her Gap fleece-and-drawstring pants and blasting out enough Tommy

Girl to anesthetize an army.

I scrabble to my feet. Click off the CD. (Not because I'm ashamed of what she's caught me listening to, just making a dramatic gesture.) "Well, thanks for giving me a minute to tidy the place up," I fling, opening hostilities.

My mum sighs. Goes.

"You'd need more than a minute. You'd need a week, paid assistance, and hire of a skip."

"This a formal visit, then?" I say frostily.

Sandi finally glances around. Do I detect a slight widening of the eyes? I've changed my domestic habits a bit lately. Arranged my bookshelf according to subject and in alphabetical order. Got rid of a loada junk off the floor.

"Oh, so that's the color of your carpet, is it?" she says.

"Did you want something?"

"Yeah. I've come about the video I caught you making this morning—you sad, pathetic *perve*!"

She plonks herself down on my chair. "A little dickey bird tells me you might have plans to show it at the camcorder club? That right?"

"I presume Natalie's been looking in her crystal ball again? Well, she's right. Can't wait. It's a hoot! They'll laugh themselves sick! Oh yeah, I'm thinking of sending it off to ITV as well. Could be talking nationwide coverage. Worldwide. Probably be a huge hit in Hong Kong."

Sandi's rows of eyelashes are so thick with mascara, they look like iron railings. Behind them her eyes are flashing daggers.

"I wanna see it."

"Ah," I sigh, "not possible."

"Why?"

Shrug. "Wiped it, actually."

"Wha-t? Think I'd believe that? Do I look like a lemon?"

"God, it was funny! Shoulda seen it. You exiting into the pond, arse over elbow . . . Swiping the Year Twelve twerp around the chops with the bag of bread—"

"The *who*?" She scowls.

"Hilarious footage, start to finish."

"So you'd never flipping wipe it, then. Wouldja?"

Here it comes, folks. Big, dramatic moment. Zoom in for mug shot of a sensitive, caring guy . . . "Decided it wouldn't be fair to show it, Sand. I was wiping away the temptation. Case I turned weak and changed my mind."

"Oh . . . ," she mutters suspiciously. "On the level?"

"On the level."

Pause. Sulky expression. "Well, you might've let me see it first."

Shrug.

Shuffling silence.

Where's her gratitude? Where's "thanks very much"?

"How about a word of thanks?" I prompt. "How about admitting you're in my debt? And so's your Mr. Maturity. Yeah. Andy whatsisname's in *my* debt!"

Sandi picks at her nail varnish, tight-lipped.

Go on, squirm. *Squirm*, Sandi Weston! Squirm your way out of this one, if you can. You're gonna have to thank me. No way around it.

There's a loud knock on the door.

My mum's head appears. "Anybody fancy a coffee and a bacon sandwich?" she trills.

I groan. I roll my eyes to the ceiling.

Brilliant sense of timing, my mum.

"Er . . . nah, thanks." Sandi springs to her feet. Dives for the door. "Gotta get back—not finished my homework—gotta dash. See ya!"

Off the hook!

I grind my teeth.

Thanks a bundle, Mum!

"*I'll* have a bacon butty," I snarl.

"If it's just you having one," says Mum "you can make your own."

Revelations

"There's another of them at the door now!" My mum's eyes are popping out on stalks. Curiosity's oozing out of every pore. She's peering into my room again, about half an hour later. "What have you been up to?"

"What does she look like?" I gasp, visualizing

164

Natalie. Wondering where's best to hide. "Did you let on I'm home?"

"Oh, she's small. Pretty. Polite. Nice little girl. Got a violin case. And yes, I did."

Emily? Phew! Flip me! Emily at my house? Why?

"Shall I send her up?"

Panic stations! My room's tidy by Sandi standards. But Emily's "Little Miss Neat and Perfect."

Mum stands watching me, arms folded, as I fling on my new DKNY T-shirt and start running around like a headless chicken. She raises her eyebrows and transfers her hands to her hips. "Shall I tell her to come back next week?"

Ha, ha!

"Remove anything that's embarrassing, fetid, or smells!" I bark.

She collapses into giggles.

Honestly, my mum is *useless* in an emergency.

I finally force the wardrobe door shut. I shove my empty mug and bacon plate under the bed. Then I grab my Febreze and squirt around the area where the plate stood, plus a few squirts into the air for good measure.

"Fascinating . . . ," Mum mutters, like she's Jane Goodall observing the personal habits of a rare species of chimpanzee.

"Send her up," I gasp.

Mum drops me a curtsy. "Yes, milord."

"Well. Emily. Hello. Wanna sit down?"

She shakes her head.

I've not seen her out of school uniform before. She's wearing jeans and a denim Diesel jacket, with a pink sweater underneath. Plus she's got some pink lippy on and there's a smudge of blue-colored eye shadow. She looks nice.

"I've come about that video," she says. Straight out. Not even blinking.

"*What?*"

I'm taken aback.

She looks so innocent standing there. How *dare* that Andy send nice little girls to do his dirty work? What *has* this guy got going for him? Year Twelve or not, he's gonna get a piece of my mind. Texted and anonymous though.

"Andy wants it. He's livid. He's heard you're planning to show it at the camcorder club. Says it'll make him a laughingstock. *And* you've caused him to wreck his new Adidas trainers that cost a hundred quid. He's not very happy about that, either."

Sharp stab of jealousy. Can afford to walk around with a hundred quid on his big, flat feet, can he? Wrecked 'em, though, did he? I control a smirk.

"Really?" I cock an eyebrow, coolly.

"*Please* don't do it!"

Oh heck. Emily's starting to plead for him now. She's good at it. Very watcheable. Got these big, soft eyes. Picture the young Charlotte Church singing something religious. Wonder if Emily can sing?

"He's a really nice boy, when you get to know him," she says. "He's a lot more sensitive than he looks."

Should I enlighten her? Tell her what was on the video? Let her know the rodent's two-timing her with Sandi?

"He's always been really sweet to me," she's going on.

Actually, this is starting to get toe curling. Gonna have to stop her before I heave up.

"Listen, Emily," I cut in. "You need to wise up. There's something about your precious Andy you oughta know." I pause. Put on a warning frown. Prepare her. Who knows—she might throw a fit. Doesn't seem like the sort that would. But you can never tell with girls. "You're not the first female that's been around here tonight, pleading for that video."

"Oh?" she says brightly. "Has Sandi been?"

My mouth drops open. "You *know* about Sandi?"

"Oh yes."

"Don't . . . *mind*?"

Emily shrugs. "Sandi's okay."

I swallow. They're prepared to *share* him? Wish I knew what flipping Andy's got. Harness it and market it and you could compete with Coca-Cola.

I hate him! Hate, hate, hate him!

"So what happened?" she's asking.

I spread my hands. "I'd already wiped it, actually," I croak.

That's set her blinking. "It was no good, then?"

"On the contrary," I boast. "It was *fantastic*. Better than any of that video rubbish you get on the TV."

I adjust to a more modest, caring expression. "Wouldn't have been fair to show it, though."

A cute, dimpled grin plucks at the corners of Emily's mouth. "Really? Ooo-oo—wish I could've seen it! I'm glad you've wiped it, but I'd love to have seen Andy making a prize prat of himself."

"You *would*?"

"Yeah. Of course. What sister wouldn't?"

I gawp. "His *sister*?"

"Yeah. Didn't you know?"

Duh! How thick can you get?

Actually, not that thick. I'm on to the personal implications of this sibling info in one big stride.

If she's the twerp's sister, means I've had my wires crossed all this time. I rewind to scene outside the music room. Emily offering apple—to *brother*. Rewind to the previous scene, in dining hall. Emily slicing up *my* toad-in-the-hole. Could it be Emily *has* got those big blue eyes on me after all?

Wow, whatddya know?

"Like your room," she's saying.

"Do you?" I smirk.

169

She nods. Starts letting her eyes roam. Glad I got rid of the bacon plate. Congealed ketchup's a real turnoff.

"Oh, I see you arrange your books by subject and alphabetically. So do I . . ."

"Really?"

"I'd heard you want to be a pilot," she adds, inspecting my model aircraft and my rehung posters of aircraft from World War II.

"Er, yeah," I say modestly. "Er, who told you that?"

She titters. Flicks her hair across her face. "Oh, some of the girls in my class were talking about you. . . ."

They were? Not *just* Emily interested in me, then? Could it be I'm a Year Eight girls' prime-for-development site and never guessed it?

"And I see you've got your bed facing the door."

"Yeah. Done a spot of feng shui. Rearranged it to catch the energy flow." (Not very effective so far. But I don't let on.)

She nods approvingly again.

Then she starts on my CD collection. I tense up.

This could be where it gets embarrassing. . . .

Actually she's not as disparaging as I'd expected. Only cringes a few times.

"Well," she says finally, "I suppose I'd better be going, then."

As I'm showing her out she hesitates. Looks up at me. "You never came to the music room . . ."

"Meant to." I shrug. "Something cropped up."

"Well, look in another time. I'm always there, both break and lunchtime."

"It's a date," I smirk, feeling really kindly disposed.

Emily blushes faintly. "See you then."

"Yeah, see you."

"'Bye!"

"'Byee!" I'm feeling so generous toward little Emily I even find myself doing baby waves at her as she trots off down the path.

Better come clean, now. Confess. *I* didn't wipe the video. My dad did. How? Fiddling around. Experimenting with expensive equipment he doesn't know how to handle.

"Oh, have I recorded over something?" he goes. "Well, it's your own fault. You should have saved a copy if it was that important."

Imagine how I feel. Frustration. Anger. Disappointment. I fill my dad in on the enormity of what he's just done. My comic video masterpiece, ruined! I rant and rave until finally it becomes clear to him that some sort of recompense is due me for this gross act of sabotage.

So that's how I came to have my math homework sorted so early on a Sunday evening.

Not that my dad actually did it, come to think of it. It was more like, in trying to explain it to him, struggling to set his rusty cogs in motion, I found I'd somehow managed to suss it out for myself.

Yeah—*I* did that math. *Me. Myself.*

Wonder if this is a Major Breakthrough?

Wonder if I've finally stepped out of the shadow of my dad's A-level Math grade—B?

Roll the drums!

Could be!

Looks like what started out as a boring old

Sunday's turned into a *momentous* day!

I think it really must've been fate that led me to the duck pond, video camera at the ready, half a ton of unleashed rottweiler at my side.

Funny how you can knock yourself inside out, trying to make your mark, to nil result. Then when you get distracted and you're not even trying at all— BINGO!

What a day! Loads of reasons to celebrate. Loads.

Only . . . Sigh.

Being a Year Eight heartthrob's all very well. . . . So's having your revenge . . . But when all's said and done, Sandi Weston's still going out with the Sixth Form. And my mum's still not washed me any socks.

Sandi Puts a Slant on Things

The following evening.

Brrring-brrring, brrring-brrring . . .

Up-and-at-'em girlie voice. "Hi, it's Sandi. Everybody's laughing about your video!"

News to me.

"Oh? Who's been mouthing off?"

"Everybody thinks it's really funny."

"They haven't actually *seen* it. Nobody's seen it," I point out. "So how can they?"

"Exactly. So I'm saved the embarrassment, aren't I? 'Cause talking about it's not the same as actually watching it, is it? You can put your own slant on things."

"Like what?"

"Now everybody knows I had a date in the park yesterday with a Sixth Former."

Groan. "That is *so* shallow! Wonder what your Sixth Former'd have to say if he knew you were broadcasting it?"

Long pause.

Sandi clears her throat. Then off she goes.

"Don't care what *he* thinks. We're finished anyway. Andy's got nil sense of humor. And he was like, really rude to me. And I've realized now . . . age isn't everything."

Deafening silence. My blood's stopped flowing.

Traffic's screeched to a halt. I swallow. I need to let all this info sink in. Stop and consider my reactions very carefully, or I could be snatching defeat from the jaws of victory. I can hear her listening, waiting for my reaction, ready to pounce on it and dissect it.

So no spontaneity. No punching the air and going yeah-yo-yea 'cause her fling with the Sixth Form's over. No. And let even the slightest spark of excitement seep into my voice and she'll claim I was. Excitement's definitely out.

She's realized age isn't everything! Hallelujah! Whaddya know? But bitter's out as well. Bitter's got a way of sounding like whining. And whining's pathetic and immature. So no flinging accusations, either.

Would a relieved sigh fit the bill? Got loadsa them. I fancy exhaling all those angst-created gasses in one almighty puff . . .

Nah.

Good old sarcasm, that's the one. Always cool.

"You mean he didn't see the funny side of you shoving him in the duck pond and wrecking his hundred-quid trainers?"

"How'd you know what his trainers cost?"

"An informed guess."

"Oh."

Pause.

"Well, thanks for wiping the video, anyway," she mutters.

Scraping of gratitude at last! And do I catch a slight note of disappointment 'cause I've given nothing away? Good.

"'S okay. Just let me know next time you've got a date with a Sixth Former. I'll put it down in my diary—Sandi Weston's publicity shoot."

"Oh . . . you!" She giggles. "At least you're always good for a laugh, if nothing else."

"Anytime, Sand," I say. "Ciao."

And I hang up first.

Yees! Cool, or what?

Can't believe I did that, actually. Sounded like she'd got more to say.

I'm definitely getting my act together. Great!

Only now I don't know which of 'em did the dumping. Or what the implications are, if any, for me. (Like, is Sandi wanting us to get back together, or what?)

Being cool definitely leaves you feeling superior. Sure leaves a stack of unanswered questions, though.

I'm chewing the carpet with curiosity.

Continuing the Winning Streak

"What do you call this?" It's my mum, shouting.

She's in the kitchen. Holding up two pairs of her knickers. Urrgh! They look so distressed somebody must've used them as floor rags, or worse.

I avert my eyes. "Nothing to do with me. Perhaps Dad couldn't find the shoe polish brush again." I titter.

"It IS you!" she thunders. "Don't deny it. They were in the washing machine. Mixed up with your socks."

Oooops! I do recognize them. They were those flattened objects stuck inside the drum. Well, I wasn't going to remove them. No wonder they look distressed.

"Yes! Your filthy socks! And you had the temperature up on high—for whites. Now all your socks have got baggy tops!"

"Does that mean I get new ones?" I ask hopefully. I've seen some really smart Burberry's that I'd like.

Appears not. "How can you make a disaster out of a simple matter like washing a few socks?"

Here's another time to stop and consider. Could be I've hit on something here. . . .

I eyeball her.

"Force me to fend for myself before I'm ready," I point out, "and you"ll have to expect the occasional disaster." Shrug. "Put me at the wheel of a racing car with no lessons and I'd probably hit a wall."

"Don't try to be a clever clogs with me!"

"Who's being a clever clogs?" Dad appears in the living room doorway. He's stretching like he's just unwound from an armchair. Crawled out to give Mum backup. Show a united parental front in the battle to promote my maturity. He fixes me with this narrow-eyed stare while Mum pours out her grievances again.

Only then Mum makes a tactical error. She waves the embarrassing evidence.

My dad's face cracks into a grin. Can't stop himself. Fatal move, Dad!

Knew it!

The grin gets wiped off double quick. By a pair of flying knickers.

Wow, good shot, Mum!

Wonder if other kids' parents act as childish as mine though? Can't picture it somehow. You'd think they'd act with a bit more dignity in front of me, wouldn't you? Set me a better example. How'm I supposed to achieve maturity when my parents still act like a couple of six-year-olds?

"You!" Mum wags a finger at me. "Don't you ever touch that machine again, d'you hear? Not until you've developed more sense. And not until you've got more *maturity* than your *dad*!"

Wow. Hear that? "Don't ever touch that machine again"! Could I actually be winning my battle against PPFS?

A plan of campaign is slowly emerging. Try this on for size: When dealing with parents, hide any little domestic skills you might acquire but don't enjoy.

Take cooking, for example. Cooking's okay, but clearing away dishes and washing up after's not. So what you do is this: you play the bungling-useless-prat card. Leave bits of food stuck on. Put things away in drawers and cupboards where they don't belong: knives in the spoon section, big plates teetering on a pile of small ones, salt with the cereal packets. Irritating little things like that. All guaranteed to send parental blood pressure soaring sky high. They'll soon find it's way less stressful and time-consuming doing it *themselves*. Be really thorough and you could end up not being trusted to do a single thing. Thereby getting yourself pampered like a five-year-old right up to the time you fly the nest.

How about that?

Trouble is, your innocence has gone. When you were a kid you just got waited on hand and foot and didn't even have to think about it. Now every time you pull on a clean pair of socks or leave a dirty saucepan lying about, chances are you've got a pile of nagging guilt to cope with.

Think I'll probably settle for the guilt, though.

Small price to pay for halting the march of PPFS.

Ric Is a Lost Soul

B*rrring-brrring, brrring-brrring* . . .

"Hi, 's Ric."

"Yeah?"

"Know how I was thinking of asking Ruth out? Well, I've changed my mind. She's got red legs."

Sigh of relief. "Yeah. Right. Narrow escape, mate! Weather-beaten. Comes of playing so much hockey."

"And she's got a red face."

"And a loud voice." I stoke the prejudice. "She'd have you under her thumb faster than . . . er, fast."

"And then Natalie comes along—"

"WHAT?" I nearly drop the phone.

"I think the finger of fate's pointing at Natalie—"

"Ric," I groan, "tell me you've not! Tell me you haven't gone and got a date with . . . *Natalie*?"

"Well, not quite," he says. "But I'm gonna try. Don't

know what you're huffing and puffing about. She's good fun. Thought it was great the way she and Louisa gate-crashed Ruth's party. And I was looking at her in French today and I felt this funny sorta 'ping' feeling. Like I'd never looked at her properly before and—"

"Don't ever look at her again!" I shout. "See her coming, turn away! Cross over! Shield your eyes! Make the sign of the cross!"

"What's up with you? What're you talking so stupid for? Not after her yourself, are you?"

"Yuck! Wash your mouth out! Where's my boiler-suit?"

"Why're you trying to change the subject?"

"I'm not. Just tell me."

"Well, my mum didn't like me in it. Said she didn't fancy sharing the house with a car mechanic. So she's giving it back to your mum."

Phew! Ric's release is imminent. Panic over.

Natalie-wise, means *I'm* exposed again, though. Think the time's finally come when I'm gonna have to sort that troublemaker out. I still blame Natalie for Sandi going off me. Bit rich when you think about it.

Influencing Sandi to drop me in favor of Year Twelve. Then chasing after me herself when she fails to cut the mustard with He of the Diabolical Haircut (I presume).

I've definitely made my mind up.

Natalie's bugged me long enough!

Tug of War

I'm striding across the playground before school. Natalie accosts me.

"Found that hair yet?" she hisses. "You're in my power till you do."

Right. Here's where things get sorted.

I stop. I fix her with a steely, fearless stare. "Look here, Natalie, that's a loada cobblers. So how about letting it drop, okay? 'S just not funny. Look at my face—I ain't smiling." (That's telling her.)

"Has Sandi stolen you back from me?" she gasps.

I sigh.

"Don't you want to go out with me anymore?" she groans.

"Listen, Natalie, we never were . . . I never . . . You never . . . Oh hi, Emily."

Just as I'm getting down to the nitty-gritty, a violin case gets shoved between us.

"See you in the music room at lunchtime?" says Emily's perky little voice. She's smiling up at me. Sweetly, but deadly serious.

A chill runs through me.

"What?" I attempt to return her smile, only mine's more like a grimace. I don't have a date with *her*. Well, not as such. Do I?

"I don't think so!" That's Natalie, hacking into my thought processes again. She's glowering down at Emily. Gives the violin case a nasty shove. "He's got a date with *me* at lunchtime!"

Hey! "I *have not*!" I splutter. "Not with either of you!"

Know what? Neither of 'em's listening.

In fact Natalie's elbowing me outta the way. She's attempting to intimidate Emily with her height. But Emily's standing her ground. And I'll swear she's visibly increased her own height two inches at least.

Suddenly they're going at it, hammer and tongs. Doing battle. Over me!

"Well, I asked him *first*," flings Emily. "I asked him last night. All my friends know he's going out with *me*. So there's absolutely no point in you asking him." (BISH!)

"Last night?" sneers Natalie. "He's been *my* boyfriend ever since Halloween. And as if he'd be so rubbish as to go out with a little squid of a Year Eight music swat like you!" (BASH!)

"You were chasing after my brother's friend Henry. And he's in Year Twelve! Same age difference!" counters Emily. (BOSH!)

Natalie picks herself up and launches into round two.

"Ha! As if he'd go out with a girl whose shoes look like her mummy chose them!" (BISH!)

"As if he'd go out with a girl who's so tasteless as to run after Henry!" (BASH!)

"As if he'd go out with—"

Oi!

Heaven help us, Sandi's turned up. Parted them

like a referee in a pro wrestling match. "Excuse me," she says, "couldn't help overhearing you from the other side of the science block. Well, you can both cut it out, 'cause for your information, he's going out with *me* again."

(*What*? 'Scuse me, have I missed something here?)

"How *dare* you?" Emily shrieks. (Wow. Emily's *shrieking*! And looking more fired up than you'd ever have guessed. What a dark horse!) "Just 'cause my brother's dumped you, you've got the nerve to think you can come bouncing back and take *him* over again? Just like that? Well, you're too late, Sandi Weston. He's moved on!"

"Yeah. Listen here," snarls Natalie, "you dropped him—*I* picked him up!"

"You did not!" squeals Emily, making ferocious jabs with the violin case. "*I* did!"

"You persuaded me to dump him for your own ends!" Sandi yells at Natalie. "You were after him yourself all along! Why did I listen to you? Well, let me tell you this: he's got more bish bash bosh up one sleeve of his jumper than those Year Twelve Twerps've got in their whole bodies! Put together!"

(*Now* she admits it!)

"If you're referring to my brother, take that back! My brother is NOT a twerp!" Emily turns the violin case on Sandi.

Sandi retreats behind Natalie. "Your brother's self-obsession's so big it would fill a stretch limo."

"And your backside's so big it wouldn't even fit on wide-screen!"

Ouch. This is getting really *embarrassing.*

Why am I just standing here, shaking my head and cringing? Am I really this "he" that's the bone of contention? If so, why've I been completely *sidelined*?

I glance around. A crowd's gathered. All years, both sexes. Oh heck! Listening to me being argued about. Unwittingly.

Guess what, though?

The few who can drag their eyes off the contestants seem to be glancing at me with a sort of respect. Tinged with . . . admiration?

How about that?

Not a scene of public humiliation, then?

More like a public demonstration that I've made it? Finally? Have achieved "It Guy" status?

Even Gary Grant's watching. He raises his eyebrows at me sympathetically. "Been there myself, pal"—that's the message.

My new status is confirmed.

Wow!

I drop the helpless, outta-my-depth look. I square my shoulders. I jut my chin. I shrug my way into my new persona. The Strongest Link. Best of Breed.

And then, having stamped my new persona on them all, I just walk away and leave them to it.

Yup. That's what I do.

Cool or what?

To be honest, this scene might seem like the stuff a guy's dreams are made of, but in stark reality— middle of the playground, early morning—it's all a bit, well . . . squirmy. Plus, if I just stand around smirking and preening, I'm in danger of looking more like the village idiot.

Fancy Sandi Weston fighting over me, though. In public. Letting everybody know she fancies me again.

Wow.

Might take her back.

But if she expects me to traipse around Boots in

future, while she fills her basket with girlie toiletries, the new me ain't going to do that anymore.

Some things have changed around here.

Sandi wanted change—well, she's got it. She can't expect to go out with a hot property and still call all the shots.

Brrring-brrring, brrring-brrring . . .

"Seeya outside Boots, after school?"

"Make that inside HMV, four fifteen. Er, don't be late."

"Okay."

She said Okay!

Wow, wow, wow!

Sandi and I are back together—and *I'm* in control!

Sacrificial Dad

It's geography before break. Mr. Moody (doubles with Drama) bounces in. He's four minutes late and bearing a stack of handouts, still hot off the press.

He shoves them at a girl. "Distribute these!

Geography field trip coming up, you lucky so-and-sos," he goes, rubbing his hands with theatrical glee and pushing the enthusiasm plug into its socket.

Groans all around.

"Just think of all the socializing opportunities," he winks. "One little problem." He surveys the room. "We're short of an extra male helper. So that's where your dads come in."

The mental retreat that greets this statement can be physically felt, like the tide rushing out.

"Come on! Come *on!*" Moody snaps his fingers, urging us back to heel. "Surely *some* of you have got dads who're still able bodied and handy with a first aid kit?"

Heads shake in denial. Lips zip shut. Eyes glue themselves to desk lids. The group unanimously tightens its buttocks.

Moody's eyes rake over us like a searchlight.

"Come on, come *on* . . ."

Suddenly *I've* got my hand up and I'm eyeballing Moody. The full glare of the spotlight's settled on me. I swallow.

"Er, do I take it that unless somebody volunteers this male-dad-type helper, the trip's *off*?"

Our eyes lock. The mental wires spring taut between us.

"Without this male-dad-type helper the trip is most definitely *off*," Moody repeats.

"And how important would you rate this trip, exactly, sir?"

"Group socializing-wise—one hundred percent. Fun-potential-wise—one hundred percent. Exam-wise—one hundred fifty percent."

His voice rises to a crescendo. "In fact, I'd go so far as to say that without this trip you could all *fail* geography. Your *entire* futures could be blighted. You could end up as *council cleaning operatives.*"

Feet start to shuffle. Furtive, anxious glances get exchanged.

"In that case, sir, I'll volunteer my dad."

Gasps all round.

Then a sigh of collective gratitude and relief goes up. I have a sensation of being surrounded by a sea of warm, quivery strawberry jelly.

My self-sacrifice has taken on heroic dimensions.

It's not heroic, though.

I'm on a roll here.

Not only am I now basking in the gratitude of my peers, I've also put Moody in my debt. Even better— just imagine the sheer delight of my dad when he learns that I'm throwing him a Dad-as-role-model bonding lifeline, at the eleventh hour. Thereby enabling him, after all, to face the future with a clear conscience—as a dad who "did his bit" in my teenage years. And if Dad disgraces himself on the field trip, there's always the sympathy vote to fall back on, isn't there?

Neat, eh?

"Er, my dad might come, if his can't," mutters Will, who's suddenly caught on.

Too late, Will. Too late! The coup is mine.

My dad'll be there. Fell hiking boots on his feet, Kendal Mint Cake in his rucksack, and his St. John's Ambulance credentials to the fore.

Never you fear.

Touchdown

Break. I spot Ric coming out of the science block, scowling. Must've been kept back.

"Hi, Ric. Fancy coming for a sticky bun?"

"Got no dosh."

My face cracks into a grin. "I'll treat you."

When we get to the dining hall, we're nearly too late. There's only two buns left. They've got our names on them, though.

I'm just reaching across to tweezer them up when Hardy Hardcastle comes in wearing his tracksuit and reeking of the sports field. He strides straight to the front of the queue. Elbows me out of the way. Snatches up *our* buns from under our very noses.

"You've got to be old and powerful to do that." He winks jauntily.

"Yeah, but you've got to be young and thin to get away with it," Ric hisses, out loud and bitter.

Hardy pretends not to hear. But I notice he pulls his paunch in as he swaggers off carrying his calorie overload. He can't stop his butt from wobbling inside the Lycra tracksuit, though.

"Looks like a semi-deflated air mattress!" I mutter.

Ric and I burst out laughing.

And suddenly—who'da thought it—we're revelling in our own immature physiques and youthful metabolism that can burn up sticky bun calories, no problem. We've still got the joys of manhood ahead of *us*. And we're certain that paunches and sagging butts are never going to be part of *our* agenda. Ever.

So, grinning smugly, we settle for a couple of Kit Kats.

No sweat.

Our time will come.

Glossary

bangers: cocktail weiners

berk: someone who lacks common sense

binned: dumped; disposed of in rubbish bin (trash can)

bish bash bosh: self-confidence and swagger

bloke: guy

bog roll: toilet paper

boilersuit: coveralls

butty: a sandwich

camp: theatrical; over the top

Deep Heat: British version of Ben-Gay, an ointment for muscle aches and pains

dosh: money

dossing: lazing about; not working

E Numbers: Number index used in European Union to measure the quantities of specific additives in food products

flipping: an exclamation

foddering: feeding

footie: short for football (soccer)

fringe: hair brushed forward over the forehead and cut short; bangs

games: gym class

gear: clothes

HAKA: New Zealand rugby

jumper: sweater

knackered: worn out; exhausted

Kwik-Fit/Kwik-Fit fitter: a British chain of automotive service shops; an employee of such a shop

lippy: lipstick

loo: bathroom

mate: friend

National Curriculum: British version of America's Board of Education

nosh: to eat heartily

phwoar: exclamation indicating sexual attraction

pint: glass of beer

pitch: athletic playing field

pong: a bad smell

Poundland: British store chain similar to the
    Dollar Store in America

prat: see "**berk**"

queue: a line, such as the lunch line

quid: unit of currency: one pound (like "a buck"
    in America)

ring: to call on the phone

scrum: a crowd; huddle

Sellotape: brand name for adhesive tape (like
    Scotch tape)

sin-binned: sidelined or penalized

strewth!: exclamation, like "damn!"

toad-in-the-hole: traditional British sausage
    dish

touchline: sideline; the bench

trainers: sneakers

Terms specific to school:

break: twenty minutes of free time between the
    start of school and the lunch period

First XV: the top fifteen rugby players who

comprise the main team, followed by the Second XV

form period: period in which attendance is taken for a form, or class

House Assembly: the period during which English pupils, who are divided into various "houses," meet to discuss house matters and sports

science/music/math block: specific wing of the building

Sixth Form: the two years, known as Lower and Upper Sixth, in which students aged sixteen to eighteen prepare for A-level exams to enter university

Year Eight: eighth grade/eighth-grader

Year Ten: tenth grade/tenth-grader/sophomore

Year Twelve: twelfth grade/twelfth-grader/senior